M000201387

PRAISE FOR
KILL MARGUERITE

"*Kill Marguerite* is a fearless romp through the post-avant wasteland of fictions both Lynchian and Homeric. Milks puts Shelley Jackson's *The Melancholy of Anatomy* through a cement mixer, grinding out tales as sure to delight as they radically defamiliarize. Here, *Sweet Valley Twins* gets a reboot finally worthy of the weird world it built. Milks is a master of the absurd grotesque, and *Kill Marguerite* is her powerful annunciation."

—Davis Schneiderman, author of *Drain* and the DEAD/BOOKS trilogy—*Blank, [SIC], Ink*

"Genre conventions are commonly thought of as restrictive rules, but in *Kill Marguerite* Megan Milks shows that these conventions can be agents of perversion, both glaringly porous and ridiculously invasive. Over the course of the book, Milks invokes and employs the genre conventions of fan fiction on, for example, Kafka's *Metamorphosis*, and then mixes in teen comedies, young adult novels, video games, choose-your-own adventure tales, epistolary novels, gothic tales, family romances, and 'traumarama' entries, until these many genres interrupt each other, parasite each other, and distort each other. The result of this romp is absurd, grotesque, parapornographic, violent, gurlesque, but most of all hilarious in a deadpan kind of way."

—Johannes Göransson, editor of Action Books and author of *Haute Couture* and *Entrance to a Colonial Pageant*

KILL MARGUERITE
AND OTHER STORIES

MEGAN MILKS

Emergency Press
New York

Copyright © 2014 by Megan Milks

All rights reserved

For information about permissions to reproduce selections from this book, translation rights, or to order bulk purchases, write to Emergency Press at info@emergencypress.org.

Design by Artsy Geek
Front cover concept by James Share
"Kill Marguerite" illustrations by Bill Ripley
"Earl and Ed" illustrations by Marian Runk

Milks, Megan
Kill Marguerite and Other Stories
ISBN 978-0-9894736-0-6
1. Fiction—General. 2. Fiction—Literary. 3. Fiction—Short Stories. 4. Fiction—Lesbian. 5. Fiction—Contemporary Women.

Excerpts of original artworks are included in this text: Tegan and Sara (various lyrics); *Ulysses*, by James Joyce; *Sweet Valley Twins*, numbers 5, 9, 12, 14, and 34, by Francine Pascal; *Choose Your Own Adventure #3: Space and Beyond*, by R.A. Montgomery; *My Teacher Is an Alien*, by Bruce Coville; *The Baby-Sitters Club #35*, by Ann M. Martin; and *Obsession*, by Lennard J. Davis.

Emergency Press
New York
emergencypress.org

987654321
First Printing

Printed in the United States of America
Distributed by Publishers Group West

KILL MARGUERITE

AND OTHER STORIES

KILL MARGUERITE

LEVEL ONE:
THE ROPE SWING

BEGIN>> So they are at the rope swing, swinging. The rope swing is this dinky little wooden seat knotted onto a long rope that hangs from a sturdy big tree branch and it swoops back and forth over Swift Creek Reservoir, and you can stand on the seat or sit or whatever. Some of the boys even climb up the rope while it's swinging because they're showoffs like that. And there is Caty in her jean shorts and old New Kids on the Block t-shirt getting Hot and Heavy with Alex on the rope swing, at least she guesses that this is what that means. They are making out with her straddling him on that little seat while they're swinging, back and forth, back and forth, over the creek, and the muddy water smell is lifting up to them every pass, making Caty think of tadpoles and crawdads and such.

If the water's not too low, you can jump off the rope swing into the creek and then swim to the creekbank. It's about a fifteen-foot drop, depending on the water level. You have to make sure to jump off at exactly the right moment because there are rocks in the wrong spots and they can bang you up good. And although Caty is a little bit worried about falling into the creek and dying, she feels okay for now with the wind swooping through her hair and Alex rubbing his tongue around the insides of her mouth. A-plus, Caty thinks, especially since Ray and

Matt and Brendan are hooting in support, and Caty can hear Kim's tinkly laughter cutting through. She knows she is doing something right to get this sort of reaction, to be bonding this way with her best friend forever who has already had a go with Brendan, and so there is this like Amazing fizzy feeling in her gut, and she thinks of all the secret-sharing she and Kim will do after this. But maybe secret-sharing is too kiddish now that they are getting Hot with boys.

So Caty starts kneading the meat of Alex's shoulder with her left hand while holding on for dear life with her right. She is surprised at how noisy it is to suck face, but then, this is her first official time. Official. O-f-f-i-c-i-a-l. Official. The school spelling bee is in two days, and Caty is her class representative. But she won't think about that now. Her eyes are closed, the air feels good, the birds are singing. It's Happily Ever After, and Caty feels safe and sweet with her man who loves her so bad, even though he's not really her man officially, just in her head when she's dreaming sometimes. He'll probably ignore her the minute they get off the rope swing, and that's fine because for boys, hanging out with girls is only okay sometimes.

Whoosh, whoosh. Back and forth.

Then the sky crashes open and flashes red. The birds scatter, screeching out portents of doom. Caty feels Alex freeze up and she opens her eyes in alarm.

"Did you *see* Nicole's bangs today?"

Fucking shit.

"I know, they were like totally vertical."

It's them, the new girls, the sisters, the evil bitch queens of the universe.

"At lunch her hair spray was like flaking off into her food. She's a fricking snow globe."

"*Dis*-gusting."

Marguerite and Shelly Thurwood of 1611 Glebe Point Road. Caty can hear the whip of Ellie's riding crop as she whacks her way through the forest. Caty can see the undergrowth wilting to protect itself as the ground trembles under the stomp of Marguerite's red Keds.

"We're surrounded by white trash," Marguerite is saying.

"*Such* white trash," Shelly agrees. Whap. She sighs. "I hate it here."

"We've *got* to get Dad to move back," says Marguerite. "He'll break down sooner or—"

"Hey y'all!" Kim rings out as they break through the trees into the clearing.

"Hey y'all!" Marguerite sing-songs back with mock enthusiasm. Kim doesn't get the sarcasm. She can be such an idiot sometimes. Since they moved here Kim has been the bitch queens' entry point into the Glebe Point Posse even though (1) no one else really likes them and (2) they make fun of Kim all the time, she just never notices. It's like, all of their neverending snickers and jeers are so totally infuriating. Caty watches in restrained fury as they come sauntering into the clearing like they own the place, all so very look-at-us, all so very we-are-the-bomb-diggity, with those looks on their faces like everything is stupid, especially you. Ellie, the younger one, twirls her ponytail and lashes at a tree trunk with her crop. Whap. Her shirt flashes Hakuna Matata and Caty's like Shit, she has the same shirt but of course it looks better on Ellie because Ellie is a ballerina and Caty is Fat, and now Caty can never wear that shirt again because Ellie owns it and Ellie is related to Marguerite and Marguerite is a two-faced hussy who has it in for Caty like nobody else.

Whoosh, whoosh. Back and forth.

Caty and Alex swing over the creek as Marguerite crosses her arms over her Girls Rule Boys Drool crop top and stops a few feet in front of where Kim and Ray and Brendan and Matt are standing. Marguerite's long blond hair is twisted into a topsytail, the kind Caty always fucks up so it ends up crooked and impossible. But Marguerite knows these things, they come second nature, along with her evil demeanor. Hey look at that. Marguerite's evil *demeanor* is *demeaning, mean,* and *demon*-like, all at the same time. Caty is going to win the spelling bee if it kills her, but this is unfortunately only a momentary respite r-e-s-p-i-t-e from the nagging fear that Marguerite is almost definitely about to ruin Caty's life again.

Marguerite saunters to the edge of the overhang and puts her hands on her hips while she watches Caty and Alex swing back and forth, back and forth, and Caty just knows she is thinking of doing something mean. But then Ray, who has a huge crush on Ellie, and who hopes he can get her on the rope swing with him soon, yells out, "Y'all! Quit hogging it!" and sidles over to Ellie and Marguerite until Alex and Caty get off. Caty breathes a sigh of relief when she is off the rope swing and out of Marguerite's line of sight. Marguerite will choose someone else to pick on today, she guesses. Praise God.

Caty's stomach rumbles, saying it's time for her mid-afternoon snack. Lunch at school is so early. So as everyone hoots and hollers at Ellie and Ray on the rope swing, Caty grabs her baloney-and-cheese sandwich from her backpack and goes off a few yards to sit down and eat it.

She is just two bites in when Marguerite in her stupid tiny crop top starts making pig noises and saying "Feed me" in a high-pitched taunt just within Caty's earshot so Caty knows she is making fun of her, but Marguerite can just shrug and say "What?" when Caty looks at her accusingly.

Then everyone laughs, even Alex. Even Kim.

And you know, Caty has had a bad day at school and she is sick of this elementary-school bullcrap and aren't they in middle school now, after all? So for once she's not going to take it any more, she's going to say something, stand up for herself, instead of just playing dumb. So she says, quietly, into her sandwich:

"Bitch."

Everyone stops. Shelly and Ray hop off the rope swing, knowing something big's about to hit. For a moment, Caty glows with pride.

Then Marguerite stomps over, rage scowled across her delicate face, and shoves Caty hard so she is flat on her back in the dirt. Mmmph.

"What'd you call me?"

Caty observes snatches of dusk through the trees.

"Someone's talking to you, fatso." Marguerite kicks at Caty's sneakers and leans over into her face. "Try again. What'd you call me?"

"Nothing," Caty mumbles and looks away.

"Bullshit, fatso." Marguerite straightens. "Hey, Shelly, hold her down. Let's pull up her shirt. Let's see her blubber. Let's see if she wears a bra for her fat little blubbery boobies." Shoot. Caty's not wearing a bra— her mom says she's too young. Still reeling from being pushed into the dirt, she protests and tries clumsily to get up—but Shelly is already kneeling on her shins and Marguerite is straddling her torso, yanking Caty's shirt up over her face.

"Aww...look at the fat baby's lumps of lard." Marguerite jabs Caty's left breast with a stick.

Caty cries out and tries again to get up. No use. Marguerite prods the other breast, then moves to Caty's stomach, poking and prodding it with the stick. Caty whimpers.

"Crybaby," Marguerite says.

Everyone laughs as Caty flails around. She is a beached whale. A shapeless turd. A fat cow. Then Riley bursts through the trees running. He leaps from the edge of the overhang to grab the rope swing in mid-air. Marguerite gets up. "Showoff!" she yells. So everyone goes over to watch Riley, leaving Caty in the dirt to pull her shirt down and breathe in deep. She sits up. They've stomped her half-eaten sandwich into a gross dirty turd. For a minute Caty just sits, holding in the tears, staring at them all as they hoot and holler at Riley, who is climbing up the rope swing while it's swinging, a dangerous, badass thing to do. Kim turns and makes eye contact, mouthing the word Sorry. Caty looks away.

Eventually she gets up, slinks over to her bike, plunks her fat ass on it, and pedals numbly away.

So there is Caty, riding her old, outgrown mountain bike furiously, all the way from the rope swing to her house, which is a pretty long way, you know, the two being on opposite ends of the neighborhood. Caty is pedaling fast as her thick legs will pedal, her purple handlebar streamers jerking violently to the rhythm of her legs. She is just one sniffle away from crumpling into ugly-crying-fat-girl face, and she wants to get home quick before she succumbs, because then the whole neighborhood will think she's a big fat crybaby, just like Marguerite says, even though Caty has been told lots of times that she is actually very mature for a twelve-year-old.

As she pedals, she passes Kim's house, which is right across the street from the Thurwoods. She can't believe Kim just stood there and let them do that to her, Caty, Kim's BFF. And Caty knows if she tries to make her feel bad about it, Kim will act like they were just having fun, why does Caty have to take things so personally all the time? Well, when did Kim get so utterly clueless. And why did Marguerite and Shelly have to move here in the first place! Caty bites her lip and stands on her pedals to make it up the big hill.

Before They moved here it was just Caty and Kim, who were like total BFFs, and everything was magic. They'd go over to each other's houses after school every day, and they'd trade stickers and build tree forts and hunt crawdads and pretend they were dogs and detectives and R&B stars. Then one day a few months ago Caty went over to Kim's house to watch *The Birds* again and found two other girls there: Marguerite and Shelly Thurwood, from Long Island, who'd just moved into the McAllisters' old house across the street from Kim. And when Caty walked into Kim's bedroom, she saw all of Kim's sticker stuff laid out on the carpet, she hadn't even waited for Caty, and Kim sitting with a smile on her face and one hand extended towards Marguerite, and in Kim's hand was—Caty still can't believe it—it was the huge limited edition Lisa Frank leopard sticker that Caty had been eyeing for months! And Marguerite didn't even have any stickers to trade for it.

Caty stood there gaping as Kim chirped, "Now you can start your *own* sticker collection!"

Marguerite rolled her eyes. "Hey, wanna make friendship bracelets?"

"Sure!" Kim didn't get the sarcasm. "I've got tons of stuff."

Caty knocked on the open door to announce herself.

Kim looked up. "Hey Caty! Marguerite, Shelly—this is my friend Caty."

Just "friend." Not "best friend forever." Caty's face fell. She fingered her half of their BFF necklace and slipped it under her shirt. Marguerite took one look at Caty and scooted closer to Shelly and Kim so there was no room for Caty in the circle.

It's been like that ever since.

And the worst is that Marguerite and Shelly are both just as skinny and little as Kim, and so now Caty is Fat, even though she's only fat just a little bit, it's just a little extra, and according to Caty's cousin June, who is a real teenager, well, she says that lots of boys like that, especially when the extra's around the bum area, which Caty's is, so take that Marguerite, you flat-assed prepubescent.

Yeah. Caty glowers at the road ahead. Take that.

Caty is being a lameass turd, Caty thinks, and decides to turn around and tell Marguerite off once and for goddamned all.

So she turns her bike around, not bothering to slow down, she is impatient for vengeance, you know, and the front tire goes off the road and snags the edge of the asphalt, oh no, and Caty saves herself by swerving to the side real quick and uh-oh, there is a minivan in her way. It is an Aerostar, going fast, looks like Mrs. Dabbieri in the driver's seat and yep, it is, as Caty's head goes right through the windshield, and one of Caty's hearts starts to tremble, and Mrs. Dabbieri is looking mighty surprised and then Mrs. Dabbieri gets bloodspattered bright red as Caty's neck is slit open by the glass.

Caty has died.

LEVEL ONE:
THE ROPE SWING

BEGIN>> So they are at the rope swing, swinging, and there is Caty again, getting Hot and Heavy with Alex while straddling him on the wooden seat.

And there are Marguerite and Shelly, sauntering into the clearing from the woods.

And Caty knows what is going to happen but she just lets it play again because she is psyching herself up to kick Marguerite in the goddamn head as soon as she gets close. So she just watches while Marguerite saunters to the edge of the overhang and glares at Caty and Alex, all so very amused, all so very what-have-we-here. And when Ray yells out "Hey y'all! Quit hogging!" Caty anticipates Marguerite's distraction and kicks her leg out furiously in Marguerite's direction, aiming to make contact with her head.

But all she gets is Marguerite's topsytail sliding silky smooth over her hi-top, and now she's losing her balance. There she goes, backward, down, off the rope swing and into the goshdarn dirt. Oof, that hurt. Kim and Brendan cover their mouths and try to hide their laughter. Alex gets off the rope swing to ask if she's okay.

Marguerite touches the back of her head and looks around suspiciously.

"She was trying to kick you!" Shelly cries, pointing her riding crop at Caty.

"Oh yeah?" Marguerite says, and stomps over to Caty on the ground.

Caty sits up and examines her scraped elbow. She pays no attention to Marguerite.

So Marguerite shoves her down in the dirt and the same scene plays out a second time: Feed me, feed me, oink, oink, oink. Caty squirming as Marguerite pokes her thick breasts and stomach, and she can't get loose until Riley flies through the clearing and distracts them.

Then Caty, forgetting all about vengeance, pulls down her shirt and gets up, brushing herself off and trying to regain her dignity. Sniffling, she walks back to the trail to get her bike and leave.

By the time she gets there, her embarrassment has turned to anger. Caty is mad at Marguerite. Caty is mad at herself.

Caty picks up her bike and Marguerite's piercing voice repeats in her mind—Feed me, Feed me. It reminds her of that recurring dream she has all the time with the popsicles in the freezer. In the dream Caty opens the freezer door and all of the popsicles, there are lots, all different colors, the freezer is full of popsicles, and they all yell at her, shrieking Eat me Eat me, and the pitch of their voices gets higher and higher and louder and louder until it's unbearable and Caty wakes in a sweat thinking her eardrums are shattered and the popsicles will kill her for sure. The popsicles, the popsicles, they scream and scream. And Caty now sitting on her bike with crumple-face wonders why doesn't she ever just slam the freezer door shut in the dream, why does she just stand there and let the popsicles scream and scream, why does she let them do that?

Shut the door on the popsicles, Caty. Shut the goddamn bitchass door once and for goddamn all motherfucker.

Caty sets down her bike. She balls up her fists and turns heel, marching back to the clearing. She hides behind a tree and listens to Kim and Marguerite practice The Ugly Song on Brendan. "You ugly. You ugly. Yo momma say you ugly." But everyone knows Brendan isn't really ugly and actually Kim has kind of a thing for him and she and Marguerite are just flirting while Shelly and Ray swing on the rope swing whoosh, whoosh, back and forth over Swift Creek.

"No, fathead, you don't clap there."

Marguerite is being loud and bossy as usual. But, Caty thinks from her spy position, we'll see how loud and bossy she is when Caty explodes through the woods to obliterate her skank ass. Caty's hands are sweating. Should she?

"U. G. L. Y. You ain't got no alibi."

Shut the freezer door! Caty zooms forward and pushes Marguerite down into the dirt. Kim backs away and Marguerite tries to get up but Caty grabs her topsytail and yanks with all her strength. Marguerite cries out in pain, then pulls Caty's legs out from under her. Caty falls, oof, on her bum, but she manages to get up before Marguerite does. Then whoosh. Shelly and Ray swing into Caty and snag her armpits with their tangle of sneakers, and now she is whooshing back and forth, back and forth over Swift Creek with them, her body hanging in the damp autumn air, her torso lodged between sneakers, and then Shelly shifts just a little because Caty's chin is digging into her shin and there goes Caty into Swift Creek Reservoir, dropped at a very wrong place to be dropped. She hits her head on a rock and there she goes, one of her hearts explodes.

Caty has died.

LEVEL ONE:
THE ROPE SWING

BEGIN>> Caty is at the mouth of the trail, thinking how she only has one life left, but lucky for her she's getting the hang of this. So Caty balls up her fists and turns heel, marching back to the rope swing like she means business. She stops a few yards away behind a tree and listens to Kim and Marguerite sing The Ugly Song to Brendan.

"U. G. L. Y…"

Caty is about to make her move but stops a minute, thinking maybe she will pray first since last time didn't go so well, even though she was This Close to kicking Marguerite's tail for good. So she looks up at the sky or the heavens or whatever and closes her eyes and prays to God, "God, please let me kill Marguerite and win back my BFF—please?" And when she opens her eyes, she sees something glinting way up in the tree above her. What's that, she wonders, and thinks maybe it's a special weapon sent by God especially for her. So she climbs up the tree quietlike trying to hold in her grunts and see, she can't be that Fat if she can climb up a tree, now, can she? Finally she reaches the branch where the shiny thing is lodged, and look, it is a rifle:

Chime! This will be easy.

Caty slings the rifle over her shoulder and slides down the trunk to the ground. She grips the gun with both hands and pauses for just the right moment as Kim and Marguerite end their cheer with their hands on their hips, all attitude, all sassified with themselves, and this has got to be the exact right moment, Caty thinks, so she screams "Bite me you bitch," and she shoots and she jumps and she shoots and she jumps again.

Wrong button.

Her cover's blown. Marguerite is whipping a grenade launcher from her back pocket, what! This is Caty's game! But Caty is figuring out her buttons and quick before Marguerite can get her first, Caty aims at the throat of the grenade launcher as Marguerite lines it up with Caty's head, and Caty shoots, BAMMMM, and the grenade launcher explodes, right in Marguerite's face, and Marguerite disintegrates into a pile of dust.

Ding-ding-ding-ding! LEVEL COMPLETE!

Caty's arms go up in slow-motion champion mode. The world fades out.

BONUS ROUND:
SIXTH PERIOD

Caty is in Science class, dissecting a frog with her partner Betty Finn. Caty is wearing turquoise jeans and an itchy sweater and her gun is stuffed in the training bra she bought after the rope swing. Next to them, Christopher Smith is popping out his frog's eyeballs and saying "Hey Caty, dare me to eat these?" And Caty's saying, "No." But he eats them anyway, after repeating more loudly his "Hey Caty, dare me to eat these?" and getting everyone else's attention, and everyone's like Ew, gross, Christopher Smith and Caty's like "[Eyeballs rolling in head]." Then he says "Hmm," and belches and waves the smell around the room, but especially at Caty.

And everyone is laughing, that ridiculous freakish kind of laugh that doesn't seem like it'll ever end, ever, and then Marguerite who is an office aide this period, enters the room and everyone just sort of stops. The guys they are all like Ohhhh Marguerite she is so Pretty, and the girls are all fidgeting like Ohhh Marguerite do you think she thinks I'm Cool? Except for Caty who knows Marguerite must be destroyed.

Marguerite hands Mrs. Gill the slip she has come to deliver, then walks back to the door. Just as everyone is going back to their frog dissections and Mrs. Gill is waving the slip of paper at Howard Grey, Marguerite slinks over to Caty and Betty Finn and leans against the lab counter with her arms across her chest.

"Hiya, Betty," says Marguerite, and Betty's all like Gee whiz, Marguerite Thurwood likes me wow! And Betty smoothes her hair and smiles and says Hi back, and Marguerite says "So, Betty," and now she has an audience, "aren't you afraid Blubberbutt here is gonna eat your frog? I can hear her stomach growling from Guidance."

And Marguerite makes smacking noises and pretends to burp before erupting into snickers. Betty looks down at her specimen's split-open stomach.

Turning to Caty, Marguerite lowers her voice. "It's you and me after school, fatty. The trampoline. So like be there or *die*." She picks up the frog by its paper towel and pushes it at Caty. "Eat me, eat me," she snickers, and after Caty takes the frog lamely, because it has been handed to her, Marguerite saunters out of the classroom, her laughter ricocheting off lockers, like MWAH HA HA, like all the evil villains in all the cartoons that have ever been made, her topsytail swishing behind her.

Something glittery catches Caty's eye. She looks at the frog and sees that its heart is bright red and beating hard and strong. Oh, goody. Caty knows what to do. She picks up the frog and eats it. Ba-da-dum-chime! It tastes like preserved swamp, but in the swallowing she has earned a new heart, so take that, Marguerite, you're dead fucking meat.

And everyone is like dumbfounded and then retardedly hysterical over Caty's public feasting, but it's way beyond what everyone else thinks now, Caty thinks. Mrs. Gill asks Caty if she's all right and Caty just glares at her, burps really hard, and waits for the bell to ring.

LEVEL TWO:
THE TRAMPOLINE

BEGIN>> The trampoline is this big old trampoline in Matt and Curtis Wheeler's backyard, and it's surrounded by woods on pretty much all sides, which is why it's so dangerous if you were to jump wrong or get pushed— you could go right into a tree, you know, and your whole face'd get slogged off by bark. It used to be fun and safe when Caty and Kim were in their heaviest BFF stage, when Kim liked Matt and Caty liked Curtis and they jumped and laughed and poked each other, and the boys doublejumped the girls to get them to go higher. Then Marguerite and Ellie moved in, you know, and that was the end of that. Everyone started getting rough and mean and tried to push each other into trees all the time, which Caty didn't like, not one bit.

But now she has an extra heart and a gun, and is dressed in her brother's camo, and so Caty is stealth magic. She decides to check out the scene before she makes herself known since she is smart like that. So she goes the back way through the woods to get to the trampoline, and tries to be quiet and not step on twigs, which are always so loud and revealing, especially when you're Fat like Caty.

So Caty is crouched low a few trees back and surveying the scene. Shelly and Kim are there, plus the Wheelers, Riley, Alex, Brendan, and Ray.

Suddenly the air beats red and the birds turn into exclamation points flying across the sky. Caty tenses. Marguerite slinks out of the Wheelers' house in black spandex ninja gear, handling some nunchucks and other ninja stuff, and Caty is like Uh-oh and Oh shit, perhaps she has underestimated her enemy.

"Oh Caty...Caty Caty fugly lady, how does your stomach grow?... Come out and fight, you fat chicken... Aww, is the fat chicken worried she'll break the trampoline?" Marguerite whooshes her nunchucks around expertlike and heck no, gun or no gun, Caty's not going in there.

She's in the process of backing away when she hears a gentle jingle coming from the action arena. Look, up there, in the tree above the trampoline, right above Marguerite's head, something glittery. Could it be... SuperPowers? Caty zooms in—yes. Lodged in a big tree branch is a jetpack.

The game has now changed entirely.

So Caty pauses and wonders how she might grab the rocket pack without Marguerite strangling her with her nunchucks. Caty stands a minute, her mind chewing hard on this dilemma. And the smell of the woods is bringing back memories of last weekend, in the woods, at night, when they'd all gone camping, Marguerite, Shelly, Kim, and Caty, so deep in Marguerite and Shelly's backyard you could barely see the light from the Thurwoods' porch. And Caty is remembering how, when she had to go to the bathroom real bad, they wouldn't let her take the flashlight, so she just went in the woods, close, but not close enough for them to shine the flashlight on her naked bum; and how they wouldn't let her back in the tent afterwards until she'd gone all the way in the house in the dark to wash her hands; and how, when she got back, there was no one in the tent, no one at all, and it was really creepy like in Unsolved Mysteries. She'd zipped herself in and waited for like an hour until she got too scared and had to pee again, she'd had a lot of Sprite, you know, and so she decided to leave the tent and go back in the house to sleep, they must have all gone in after her, that was it. So she unzipped the tent zipper and cautiously stepped outside. And as soon as she was out they all flew at her from nowhere, howling and laughing and screaming. And Caty was so scared she shrieked and peed her pants and then they made fun of her all the rest of the night and made her sleep in the bathroom, on the toilet, just in case.

And she had. Why had she done that? Why hadn't she just...

"Caty Caty fugly lady...."

"AWWARRWAWR!" Caty rips toward the trampoline with vengeance. In her rage she is blind to the fallen branch in her way and she trips over it and slips on the wet leaves, and wow, that was a bad entrance, like the worst entrance she could have made. One of her hearts flashes. Caty is down.

Marguerite swings around and sees Caty in the woods struggling to get up. She pulls her arm back, then throws. Here come the nunchucks, straight for Caty's neck.

Durnnh-durnnnh.

Caty has died.

LEVEL TWO:
THE TRAMPOLINE

BEGIN>> Caty crawls toward the trampoline the back way again. Shelly and Kim are already there, plus the Wheelers, Riley, Alex, Brendan, and Ray, and there's Marguerite slinking out of the Wheelers' house in black spandex ninja gear, handling some nunchucks and other ninja stuff.

Caty clocks the SuperPowers sitting in the tree and deduces that the only way to get them is to use the trampoline. She breathes deep for a minute and tries to develop a strategy. She will play dumb, she decides. They're used to that. So Caty steps forward and announces herself with her hands up, and everyone ripples with excitement. She hears Brendan bet Alex loudly that she won't last two minutes, but she ignores him, breathes deep and smart and asks Marguerite with much humility if she can please please jump on the trampoline just for a few minutes to warm up, please.

Marguerite thinks for a minute. "Fine," she says. "Just try not to piss your panties."

So Caty steps on the wooden block and then onto the trampoline and tests it a little. She does some dumb stretches and doesn't give a crap that they are all mimicking her in their outer-trampoline circle, she's going to get her jetpack, they'll see. She jumps and she jumps and she jumps, and then she jumps high enough to grab the branch below the jetpack and pull herself up, it is not a graceful maneuver since she has very little upper body strength, but darned if she doesn't do it, grunting all the way, and look, there she is, up in the tree in reach of her goal. Caty grabs the rocket pack and tries to put it on. A low blare sounds in her ear. Huh. She can't seem to—oh. She pulls her rifle out of her bra and stashes it in a bird's nest, then tries the jetpack again:

Chime!

Caty finds herself angling forward while the chatter below speeds up to match the accelerated soundtrack tempo. Now Caty is SuperRocketrix, and Marguerite is in big trouble.

Caty glances down to see The Enemy scrambling onto the trampoline and huffing and puffing like one of the indignant blowfish in Caty's brother's collection of dead fish and sharks.

"Uh!" Marguerite lets out and stares up at her. Caty grins from her tree branch, raises a fist, and she's off and zooming away.

She is determined to get a handle on her new powers before putting them to the test, so she tries out SuperSpeed, then aerial somersaults. She practices landing by stomping on clouds and unleashing tufts of white fuzz that rain down on her enemies.

She's ready.

Swerving away from Marguerite's flying nunchucks, Caty zooms down and lands in a somersault on the trampoline, the impact leaving Marguerite off balance so she falls hard on her bum. Marguerite bounces on the trampoline once, twice, three times, and Caty's back up in the air showing off her new and impressive acrobatic moves, like aerial somersaults and high kicks at SuperZoom speeds.

Marguerite manages to get herself upright again. "Come down and fight, you fat bitch!" she screams.

"Why don't you come up here?" Caty taunts.

Marguerite spouts samurai stars from her mouth and Caty leaps and dives in and out of clouds to protect herself. Caty says, "Hot dang Marguerite you really know how to push my buttons," and she says it bored-like and in control, like a supercool superhero named SuperRocketrix should.

But enough with the small talk. Shut the freezer door! Caty folds herself into SuperSpeed torpedo form and zings toward Marguerite, fist-first, kerplow, right in that precious evil face. Marguerite's eyes tremble as Caty's knuckles drive into them.

Marguerite is down.

Caty regroups. Her body flickers as she flies up and into a SuperPower Somersault and then Thunk, she lands powerfully, kneesdown on Marguerite's stupid head, which ruptures on impact, leaking all of the slimy spaghetti strands that were her thoughts and feelings.

Ding-ding-ding-ding! LEVEL COMPLETE.

Caty throws her arms up in champion mode, relishing her easy win and the proud look on Alex's face as he cheers for her, for Caty, and even mouths "I love you," as Kim looks on approvingly. So she is totally not ready for Shelly, who comes flying at her, trying to slice up Caty's face with her fingernails. The world fades out in time.

BONUS LEVEL:
AT HOME

Caty goes home and eats her dinner and her dessert and tries to persuade her mom to drive her to school tomorrow because she is afraid of the bus stop but she Has to go to school because tomorrow is the Spelling Bee, and she cries into her brownie when her mom says no. Why is Caty so upset, Caty's mother asks, and Caty blubbers about the mean girls in the neighborhood and how they'll kill her and stuff. And Caty's mom says, "Don't be so dramatic." She turns up the TV volume. "Fine. I'll drive you. Have another brownie."

Caty marches over to the kitchen counter where the brownie pan is, and look, a slick red heart is beating thu-thump in the middle of the pan. Caty claws it out of the pan and swallows it whole. Ba-da-dum-chime! New life.

LEVEL THREE:
THE SPELLING BEE

BEGIN>> The day of reckoning. Caty is about to face off with Marguerite, Ray, and six other spelling bee contestants, three from each grade. Caty has worn a skirt for the occasion and looks Fatter than usual because she is hiding her rocket pack under a hooded sweatshirt.

As Chester Middle's student body floods the cafeteria, the nine contestants take seats in the front of the room. The other students sit on plastic circles and impatiently turn this way and that, bumping into each other on purpose. The judges, Ms. Moore and Mr. Smith, are seated in blue chairs facing the contestants.

The cafeteria stoplight turns red and bleats a loud siren noise. The students hush, and the contestants are introduced. Marguerite's applause is twice as much as everyone else's. At this, Caty scowls.

The bee begins.

Sixth-grader Harvey Jones is out first, after skipping the second d in "hundredth." Then Ray on "subtle," and Troy Li on "schism." Caty flies through without difficulty. "Suffice." "Judgment." "Aptitude." No sweat.

Time is moving fast. The game seems to be speeding up. Pretty soon it's just Caty and Marguerite at the front of the room. No surprise. Marguerite has gotten all the easy words.

Caty glares at her nemesis. Marguerite returns it, eyeballs flashing red.

It's Caty's turn.

"Liaison," Mr. Smith overenunciates. "The Secretary of State acts as liaison between the United Nations and the president of the United States. Liaison."

"Liaison. L-I-A-I-S-O-N. Liaison." Hrmmph. Caty leaves the podium, flicking her nose in the air and walking haughtily past Marguerite to her seat.

Marguerite gets "candor." Caty gets "perceptive." Marguerite gets "eight."

Caty is getting pretty steamed at how easy Marguerite's words are. So after correctly spelling "memoir," Caty stomps on Marguerite's foot as she walks by. Marguerite winces and returns Caty's glare but otherwise doesn't crack.

Ms. Moore pronounces Marguerite's next word slowly. "Scalpel. We dissected the frog using a scalpel. Scalpel."

Marguerite smiles confidently at the judges. "Scalpel. C—,"

She gasps. Caty gasps. She hovers over her seat, ready to correctly spell "scalpel" and move forward to win it all.

"I mean S." Marguerite regains her confident smile. "S-C-A-L-P-E-L. Scalpel." She beams at the judges.

Ms. Moore and Mr. Smith cover the mic and deliberate. After a moment, Mr. Smith smiles at Marguerite and says, "That is correct."

Caty's jaw drops. Correct? She can't believe it. "Not fair!" she shouts. "This is so not fair!" She pushes her chair back and stands up. "She misspelled it!" Now she's next to Marguerite at the podium, yelling down at the judges. "Once you misspell something, you can't go back and pretend you didn't!" She jumps up and down. "This is bullcrap! I demand a recount!"

"Shut up!" Marguerite pushes Caty to the side. "Shut up! Shut up!"

"You shut up!" Caty pushes back and turns again to the judges. She stamps her foot. "This is a total inflammation of the rules!"

"Caty, calm down," Mr. Smith says in earnest. "You can still win."

"But I already won! You don't get second tries in spelling bees!"

"We have made our decision, Caty," Ms. Moore snarls. "Now take a seat."

"But she got it wrong! Tell her she got it wrong!" Caty is so busy shouting she doesn't see Marguerite pull a spiked mace out of her back pocket and swing it straight over and into Caty's skull.

Durnnnh-durnnnh.

Caty has died.

LEVEL THREE:
THE SPELLING BEE

BEGIN>> Now it's just Caty and Marguerite with Marguerite behind the podium.

"C—," Marguerite starts and then gasps. "I mean S."

Caty scowls as the judges give Marguerite the nod, but is determined to restrain herself this time. She won't be a whiny baby. She'll win the spelling bee anyway.

Caty's turn. "Recipe." Easy.

At this point, the student body is becoming bored. When Marguerite stands up again, someone, probably Shelly, starts cheering, and soon everyone has joined in, cheering and whooping for Marguerite until Ms. Moore activates the stoplight siren to get them to shut up.

Caty grits her teeth. This is her game! She should be the popular one.

As Marguerite steps smugly up to the podium, this time Caty takes a good long look at her. Who is Caty fooling? Nobody cares about Caty. Nobody cares about Caty's personal vendetta, the score she has to settle. Alex doesn't really love her, and Kim is a stupid BFF anyway. Anyway, the only way to kill Marguerite is to become a better Marguerite than Marguerite is. Does Caty really want that? Yes. No. Maybe so. Yes. No. Maybe—

Marguerite sits down in a huff. She has misspelled "sauna."

Now is Caty's chance. If Caty spells "sauna" correctly, and the word after that correctly too, she will win the school spelling bee and move on to the county bee, her next achievable life goal. She can do this. She's going to do this.

She leans forward into the mic and opens her mouth to spell.

"Sauna. S-A-U—"

A whoosh sounds behind her. Caty spins to find Marguerite brandishing an executioner's double-bladed ax. What! Caty springs to action, jumping back against the podium and trying to activate her rocket pack—but she can't find the power switch under her hooded sweatshirt. Frantic, she scrambles behind the podium. Marguerite approaches from the other side while Ellie rallies the crowd: "Kill Caty! Kill Caty!" The entire middle school population, Caty excluded, roars as one.

Caty tries to yank off her sweatshirt but shit, now it's stuck around her head, just like in the locker room when she tries to change lightning-fast and ends up twisted and—focus! Focus! She pulls the sweatshirt off, only to feel several hands groping for the straps of her jetpack. No! She one-eighties, kicks a leg out and trips all three enemy combatants. But behind them, hundreds of other students are amassing, seconds away from eliminating her in any number of gruesome ways.

Jet away, Caty! Get the heck out of there! Caty is groping for the ON switch when Marguerite shouts close in her ear.

"Die, you fatso! Lose some weight, get a boyfriend, and die!" She raises the ax.

Not fair, Caty thinks as it catches her neck. So not fair.

GAME OVER.

SLUG

Patty will ask her date to walk her to the door. Patty will play I'm Frightened and Scared to be Alone in the Deep Dark Night. Of course he will accompany her, despite the drizzle. He will be happy to. Delighted. Then Patty will push him up against the door so that he's straddling the doorknob, so it's pressing into his asscrack, and shove his shoulders back, hard, and suck his tongue, hard, and rub his crotch, hard, and push his arms up and over his head and hold them there so that he is her prisoner. It is a good thing she wore her bitch boots tonight. It is a good thing she dressed prepared. She will take out her pocketknife and flip up the knife part and she will tickle him with the blade, slowly, deliberately, while he is still clothed, and she will increase pressure as she moves the knife down from his sternum to his pelvis. His stomach will retract involuntarily. She will press into it more. The flat side of the blade. This is foreplay, pre-foreplay.

She will unlock the door, swing it wide, and step back, return to I'm Frightened and squeak, It Looks Like There Could Be a Burglar. Won't You Please Check? I'm So Scared. He will play along, say It Would Be My Pleasure to Check for the Burglar. Stay Behind Me. Stay Close. And he will grab her wrist firmly and push her behind him, stroking her wrist suggestively. It will be nice.

Patty's date works hard to clear his throat. The first try miserably fails. He tries again, succeeds, changes the car radio to smooth jazz. Unbearable. Patty uncrosses, then recrosses her legs, begins to clench and unclench her thighs under her plain black skirt.

Patty is a wicked schoolgirl with an SM fetish. Underneath her plain black skirt is a honking big strap-on (she makes a note to self: purchase harness and dildo, a formidable dildo). At her command he will get on his hands and knees and enjoy the rug burn, you pathetic motherfucker. Patty is a vicious cunt in bondage gear, with a whip and not afraid to use it, slave. Patty likes to be tied up, chained up with needles through her nipples, getting burned to bloodblack with cigarettes and branding irons. Patty enjoys biting and being bitten, hard, like starved vampires. She also enjoys: bestiality; triple, quadruple penetration; and feverish, drugged-up sex parties. Sex parties have lots of drugs. What kinds of drugs will Patty's sex party have? Patty is in the middle of being gangbanged, which means violence and overwhelming numbers of cocks at once. Patty is the one with the cock, and she is making him eat it, swallow it, gag.

"You're not giving me much to go on," he says.

He has been talking all this time.

She will smear his forehead with menstrual blood, then slice a line in his lower abdomen and rub her face in his blood and guts. And shit. Shit will be smeared everywhere. She will hang him upside down, ankles chained together and thighs caked with shit. She will leave him there with her formidable dildo in his asshole and slashes in his heels so he cannot walk when she unties him. She will be ruthless and loyal. After she slashes his heels, she will check in with a Baby, Are You Okay? Tell

Me You're Okay, and take out his gag so he can say so. Then she will shove the gag back down his throat, kneel before him and masturbate where he can see her, inches from his nose and mouth.

Patty shrugs, smiles lazily over at him, lost in her dreaming.

His tongue in her mouth is slithery and warm, then a lifeless slab of muscle to her weak response. Fumbling and finally dead. Retracted. Suck.

Patty clenches and unclenches her thighs, faster, faster, until she is done.

When she is done, she thanks him, they should do it again sometime.

Then she slams the car door and hurries through the rain to her apartment building, stepping on a slug that's sprawled out to suck in the moisture. Ugh. That squishes. She scrapes the slug-guts off on the doorstep and lets herself inside.

In the kitchen, Patty grabs a used glass and fills it with filtered water. Gulps it down. Stands there with her fingers on her lips, thinking he wasn't so bad. She could have been nicer. She could have tried harder. Made something happen. But what had he looked like? She remembers the nervous gurgling in particular. The meek way he cleared his throat. The tapping on the steering wheel, anxious, impatient.

She had made him impatient. That's funny. She had had an effect. He probably would've been too safe in bed, anyway. He would've wanted her to act like a girl.

Everyone is always too safe. Probably. What do normal people do?

They take off their shoes and makeup, and go to bed.

Patty takes off her shoes and makeup and goes to bed. Patty has not closed her window, despite the drizzle, which has now turned to rain. There is a lot of rain. It is raining hard. The rain is hard. Hard rain. Getting harder. The rain is getting harder and harder until it is too hard for anyone to handle.

Patty close the window! Patty close the window!

But Patty does not close the window.

Once, a long while ago, Patty was in love, with a man she met online. He had responded to an ad, or she had responded to his, and they had had a feverish exchange in which each had confessed her or his own and encouraged one another's perversities. He wrote every morning; she responded dutifully before retiring for the night. In their emails, they would each describe her or his every desire in obsessive detail, carefully crafting fetish after fetish with the intent to elicit the most violent desire and intrigue from her or his reader. For Patty, masturbation had never been so good.

After a time, they began to write erotic stories for each other. Patty wrote rottingdonquix a story after Story of O, in which O grew a cock and turned the tables on her Master, reducing him to the most obsequious and pathetic of slaves. Rottingdonquix responded with a story inspired, she found out later, by Masoch, in which his Venus was not so much wearing furs as she was covered in fur, for she was a vampiric werewolf who feverishly desired to suck the blood from the narrator's cock. Patty had written him another story, in which Bataille's bull's eye is passed back and forth from orifice to orifice until finally, in the midst of passionate intercourse, it bursts in the protagonist's throbbing cunt. He wrote back with an overwrought masturbation fantasy revolving around an onyx engagement ring. Upon reading it, she experienced the strong stench of rotten eggs, and could not bring herself to reply.

Weeks passed.

One day, missing the thrill of rottingdonquix's emails, Patty wrote him with the suggestion that they meet in person. He agreed.

He was fat, and ugly. She left with a sneer on her face.

That was the end of love.

Patty is in her bed masturbating. She has tied her date up with fishing line that cuts into his skin, leaves blood blisters pooling subcutaneous. She does the same with his cock, which is always fully erect, engorged even, then kneels in front of him, makes eye contact, and extracts her tongue slowly, torturously, until the tip just touches the head of it. He moans behind his gag. Saliva gets stuck in his throat and he tries to clear it, takes two tries, three, is perpetually clearing his throat. Patty's tongue has not moved from its tentative perch on the tip of his cock. Then she lurches forward to wrap it around the head while grabbing the ends of the fishing line with her hand and tugging, gently, gently, until he comes. He comes five more times as she frees his cock from the fishing line.

Patty does not come, because Patty's fantasy is dumb. Mindless SM drivel. Patty can do better.

She tries again.

Patty is masturbating. Patty grows a cock and it extends, fully engorged and throbbing with sensation. Patty's cock extends and extends, quivering in the air it is exposed in, then slowly curves backward and into her cunt. Patty's cock tentatively probes her cunt before beginning to fuck it, first leisurely, then hard, pummeling it in sync with the hard rain outside.

Patty's cock and Patty's cunt come at the same time.

Patty comes.

Patty drifts off.

Patty still has not closed the window.

Tap, tap. Tap.

Slug hangs down from the top of the window, suctioning his wet body, his enormous foot, to the exterior pane. There is a loud and sustained squerk as Slug navigates the window pane at his infuriatingly slow pace.

Patty stirs from her half-sleep.

Two sets of tentacles probe the glass.

Tap, tap.

Tap.

The incoming air is cold and moist. Patty stirs again, shivers. Her nipples tighten.

Slug's tentacles fidget impatiently as they work to gauge the size of the opening. The open window is not wide enough for Slug's impressive girth, but Slug is both lubricated and stretchy. He begins the process of entering her room.

Patty blinks.

Slug is six feet of pure muscle struggling to get through her window. Slug is a rippling lump of skin shimmering with beads of rain on top of a more general wetness. Slug is multicolored, translucent skin, eyeless, faceless, hairless. Slug's intricate underbelly is lined with undulating muscles that tremble against the pane, excreting stickiness, excreting slime.

Patty, torn between horror and desire, cannot bring herself to look away.

By now Slug has pushed a quarter of his body through the window, attaching himself to the other side of the glass. He pulls himself farther forward, inch by thick inch, up the glass until his full length is inside. A pause, a shudder of slick skin, before he continues. He crawls along the wall, staining it with his wet trail as he nears her bed. Hanging down, he fills her nostrils with the smell of fresh soil. His tentacles toy with her hair.

Slug curves toward her, his back end vertical, attached to the wall, his front end suctioning itself to her shoulder, kneading her skin with his underbelly: like an introduction, like saying hello.

Patty sucks in her breath.

Hello.

He twists toward her head. Soon there is mucous creeping through her hair. His front end gropes her forehead, sticky lubricant oozing into her brows, clumping her eyelashes together, choking her nasal passage with a swamp musk. She opens her mouth to breathe. He enters, gropes around, sucks on her tongue noisily with the front portion of his foot, and pushes forward until her throat closes up and rejects him. He pulls himself out, with reluctance; works his way to her torso. Past her chin, along her neck, he slurps noisily, slowly, taking his time. The bedsprings bark. As he moves forward, he shoves her camisole down, the thin straps breaking, and flattens both breasts with his weight, his belly gripping and releasing her nipples rhythmically. She finds herself making soft gurgling sounds deep in her larynx. Slug gurgles Slug's reply.

Then he slugs himself down, less leisurely now, hugging the curves of her abdomen, his tentacles seeking her tunnel. Slowed by an unruly nest of hairs, his lubricant smooths the way, and—at last—he probes her slit, first tentative, then with force. He inches forward, nudging her thighs apart.

Patty's hands claw at the sheets. The wind rustles trees outside. The wind enters the room triumphantly, amplifying the scent of swamp that is beginning to suffocate Patty.

Slug surges forward, stretching himself taut, easily eight feet long, digging, digging as deep as he can, the bed creaking with every insatiable thrust. Lodged inside her vulva, his front half shifts to suit her, curving back and downward. The rest of his body, resting on her torso, kneads her flesh raw. Under his weight, she struggles to further open her thighs. It is difficult—he is massive, his skin so slippery—but she needs to show him: more, please more. She wants all of him. Slug manages to pull a few more inches of his body inside, his trembling underbelly attacking her canal from all angles, speeding its tempo to frantic bursts. Faster. Harder. Her muscles tense. Faster. Harder. Almost. Slug gently chews the insides of her cervix, bringing her to excessive climax. Patty arches, kicks, sucks in so deep she nearly swallows her tongue.

The room is heavy with dampness. Slug slows to a hum. Then he extracts himself slowly, the suction stubborn, painful to break, and rests on top of her, his underbelly engulfing her whole body in its folds.

Slug has crushed Patty. Patty has died.

Slug kisses Patty. Slug kisses Patty until Patty can't breathe. Slug is in her nostrils and in her mouth. Slug's mucous drips down her throat and fills her lungs. Slug's mucous fills her body.

Patty is drenched in Slug. Her eyes are slimed shut, her hair slimed into new skin. Her face is slimed into an amorphous blob. Patty tries to move, but Slug's weight prevents her. She chokes a little, learning how to breathe again.

His work done, Slug releases her and crawls onto the wall behind her. He creeps back over to the window and perches, his head turned towards her, his tentacles dancing. He emits a gurgle. It seems to mean Come With Me.

Though she cannot see the limbs that are no longer there, Patty understands that her body has changed. She rolls onto her belly, finding that she can feel where she is with two sets of tentacles attached to what used to be her face. She tries to talk but can only gurgle back.

Slug nods: he understands.

Patty follows Slug through the trees behind her building, their slime smoothing them over wet leaves and limp twigs, over thin gravel, the occasional rotting pine cone, until they come to a heavy dampness under a half-fallen tree trunk. Slug turns back and nudges her playfully, his tentacles fondling hers. Then he leads her up the trunk and out onto one of its outstretched limbs. There they mate, Slug showing her how to wrap around his length as he wraps around hers, so that they are a DNA strand, a corkscrew, hanging down from the limb on one rope of slime. It is easy, like love, this full-body writhing. For a long while they are content to lick each other, lapping up one another's slime and producing more in its place.

This is the wettest Patty has ever been. Her body is in full tremble, every pore of her skin secreting slime, every nerve channeling excitement.

Suddenly she feels a new sensation: her cock is beginning to protrude translucent from her mantle to wrap around Slug's protruding cock, its sensitivity heightened with every fondle of the wind. Like their bodies, their cocks writhe around each other until they are intertwined. Then their cocks begin to expand, throbbing and massive, together forming an intricate flower that dangles down from their hanging bodies.

Patty and Slug tighten their embrace further and further still, in sync with their pulsating cocks. Tighter, tighter, tighter; their cocks throb, begging for release. Finally they ejaculate, each fertilizing the other in an extended excessive climax that ends all time and thought.

Patty is dizzy. Patty is exhausted. Patty has more work to do.

Because Slug's cock is stuck in Patty's cock, Patty must begin to chew it away, being careful not to chew off her own cock in the process. As Patty gently chews, Slug writhes around her body and gurgles in pleasure, in pain. When she is done, Slug drops down and sprawls on the leaf-matted forest ground for a moment, recovering. Then he creeps away.

Now Patty is alone, dangling precariously from the tree limb. She tries swinging herself over to the trunk but, fatigued, cannot build momentum. Like her lover, she allows herself to fall from the rope of slime to the soft ground. Though the fall is not long, the impact stings. Her skin, she supposes, is still sensitive.

Here Patty rests. What will Patty do next?

DIONYSUS

Age matters little for immortals. When I met Dionysus, I was twenty-four. She was old.

We met at an after-hours club. She caught my eye or I caught hers. Her eyes were glittery and wise. She came over and laughed. I felt good.

When Dionysus laughs, it's an all-devouring laugh, as though she is swallowing you down. It's a fearless, monstrous laugh. You must trust her to hack you back up.

Around bars and in streets, in alleys, Dionysus swirls, administering the night. She blurs the edges of people, her own borders smeared.

I tend to maintain myself. So we were in love.

*

When Zeus killed her mother, Dionysus was still in the womb. Zeus killed Semele by showing her all of himself. He sewed Dionysus into his thigh.

Zeus is a god of gods. He has also birthed a child from his head.

Dionysus has failed to live up. She serves the carnival more than she rules it. Her people command her, texting and calling, insisting she show until she does.

"I don't want to go," she'd complain, tossing the phone down and stretching in bed. "It's so much work. I'd rather stay here with you." She'd yawn, rub my back. She'd cough up mucus and swirl it in her mouth, chewing before gulping back down.

"So don't go. We could..." In truth, all we did was watch television.

"Come with me," she whined, wrapping her legs around mine. "Then I won't have to stay out so late."

In the final month of Dionysus' incubation, Zeus' jealous wife tried beating the fetus dead with an urn. While Zeus and Hera fucked their make-up fuck, Dionysus moved inside her father's thigh.

In an act the physics of which I don't understand, Zeus birthed Dionysus in the bed he shared with Hera. I imagine he unthreaded the thread that attached Dionysus to his thigh. Possibly, contractions and labor occurred.

Upon her release into the world, Dionysus scrambled over to suck the breast of her father's wife. She sucked with mighty, toothless gums. Hera, delirious, came.

Dionysus crawled from Hera's empty breast. She seized Hera's glass of wine. Dionysus drank, and drank.

"You know I don't like seeing you drunk," I said, pulling away. When she swirled around bars and streets, she forgot about me. It hurt.

She snorted. "What do you mean? I'm always drunk. I could use a beer right now. Just kidding. Ha. No, I'm not." She might stand on the bed and do her inebriated court jester routine. If I didn't laugh, she'd do a grotesque striptease. If I didn't laugh at that, she'd straddle me and make stupid faces. For a time, withholding laughter was my most effective power ploy. This worked until she resorted to merciless, profoundly unfair tickling.

*

Things became smeared. I had to keep reminding myself that Dionysus could live off of coffee and cigarettes and alcohol. I couldn't. Dionysus could bike through red traffic lights, yipping, without fear. That didn't mean I should follow her.

Dionysus could also bike home drunk and take a spill, a mistake even a god could make. Then she'd really need me.

She might need me to pick her up in a cab, for instance. She might need me to know where she lived. She might have lost her keys again; she might need me to break down the door. She might be so upset by the damage, she'd need me to get the broom. She might whisk the wood shards this way and that; she might need me to make her stop. She might threaten to throw a punch at me then, her eyeballs shivering in their sockets. She might need me to go over it all the next day. She might need me to describe it and laugh.

*

Maybe her glory would have killed me, I think sometimes. If she'd shown it. Maybe I'll call her. Then I reread her last text: her pee smells like Southern Comfort, and am I ever going to talk to her again?

Our last night involved me showing up at a bar to escort her home. She wouldn't leave. Her people were egging her on.

"Stop it, stop it," she pushed me away. "You're no fun. I want to have *fun*," she slurred, head rolling around on her neck. "I could *die* tomorrow." She flicked at me as if it would make me go away, then walked unsteadily to the bar.

She'd already been cut off, I guess, so she was taking people's drinks right out of their hands. I grabbed her around the waist and pulled her away. I felt like her parent. I felt like a security guard. I felt dangerously, violently angry. We swayed and scrambled like a disoriented crab. Outside she started crying. "Stop yelling, stop yelling," she yelled. I stopped. She grabbed my t-shirt and pulled me in toward her. I softened. She pulled up my shirt so it formed a bowl. Then she puked in it.

TOMATO HEART

It was a cool day for July, a healthy breeze keeping the heat at bay, and I had immersed myself in a matrix of tomato vines, breathing in the vine-ripe aroma and enjoying the yellow-to-red rainbow of garden fruit, when I saw a man several yards away. Silhouetted by the sun, he looked like an emaciated Giacometti, until I took a few steps forward; with the sun no longer swallowing him, he was just tall, nothing special. I watched him reach up, yank off a tomato, and chomp into it with authority, the juice squirting out upon impact and leaking down his chin with a vengeance.

He shifted and saw me. He offered me a bite.

I accepted. It was a fireball of a tomato, delicious, its tang flooding our mouths and trickling from our lips down to our chins, tickling our necks, tingeing our white T-shirts pink at the collars. It could have been just another tomato on a vine, stuck there round and shiny, swelling, waiting to be plucked and eaten, with brothers and sisters just as ripe, just as ample. But this tomato was extraordinary. I'd never tasted anything so rich. The stranger and I surveyed each other coolly as we chomped, and I felt the beginning of something, I didn't know what exactly, take root in my body.

I love tomatoes. His name was Paul.

On our first date we went to Mama Mia's, a Ninth Street hole in the wall. Paul's idea. They knew him there. I imagine he wanted to impress me with his capacity for making quaint friends like Guillermo and Estelle, the septuagenarian owners of the place. They embraced him heartily and gave me an affectionate once-over with eyebrows raised, I believe in impressed approval. At the time, I was charmed: He likes elderly Italians. He is perfect.

We had just fallen into the rhythm of a smooth tête-à-tête when our salads were served, striking us silent with their opulence: a generous array of sliced tomatoes arranged upon rippling leaves of romaine with grated mozzarella sprinkled on top. O! And a creamy Italian sauce to die for. I looked at Paul and smiled. Paul smiled back. My heart bubbled with joy as I plinked a tomato slice into my mouth and chewed. I looked at him chewing on his tomato slice as he looked at me chewing on my tomato slice, and I knew this relationship would last.

He had felt it, too, he said many months later, when we remembered with fondness that first date, the first of many such dates, many such tomato-filled salads followed by traditional Italian dishes and slow walks along the river. He was a talker, oh yes, fond of sweeping declarations and eloquent with his hands; our favorite topics were gentrification, environmental racism, urban art, and tomatoes. I love tomatoes. Since the day we met so gloriously amidst the tomato vines at the farm, we had been back to Mama Mia's twenty times at least, enough for Guillermo and Estelle to know us and give us dessert on the house from time to time, usually when we were arguing, which naturally became more frequent as time wore on.

He took me back to Mama Mia's to propose. Not marriage, but a partnership. A committed partnership. Guillermo brought out our salads, and Paul brought up that first date, that moment when we had gazed at each other with forks mid-air and plinked tomato slices into our mouths simultaneously. He claimed to have known right then, right there, that we would make it. We would commit to one another, grow old together. Darling, he said, will you be my life partner?

I looked down at my salad. He had jumped the gun a little, I thought. I didn't want to think of such things; I wanted to plink a tomato slice into my mouth and savor its garden flesh. But looking at him looking at me like that, my heart surprised me, thumping like it wanted out, like it wanted to jump right out of my chest and nestle inside his. Our hearts would grow old together. We were in love.

So I looked up and said, yes, darling, yes, I will. Paul let out a huge breath and reached for my hand. We clutched each other's hands and smiled, our eyes glistening, then kissed each other lightly over the table. I was glad then that I hadn't started in on the Male Answer Syndrome baiting, a game I'd picked up from one of our femarchist friends and grown fond of over the course of our relationship. Paul might have reneged, which, by the way, should be pronounced with a soft 'g' because it sounds better and more appropriate that way. Paul always rejected my pronunciation-as-use theories of language. I have to get them in when he's not listening.

That night we had a long bout of polite sex and then we went to sleep. When I woke up, it was early morning, and my chest was rattling noisily. Something felt wrong inside me. I was numb on one side, and my chest was swelling visibly, as though my rib cage was expanding. I must be having a heart attack, I thought. Exciting, and highly unusual for a woman my age—but I have always been special. Then I started coughing uncontrollably, so hard I feared I'd hurl up my esophagus. That was when Paul woke up, alarmed, and started whacking me on the back, saying are you all right, darling, are you all right, and, should I call the hospital, darling, I'm calling the hospital. He made for the phone. I batted his arm away.

By that point, the skin between my breasts had begun itching uncontrollably, and I couldn't help but scratch. I scratched and scratched, digging deep with my fingernails until, abruptly, I tore through my skin—it wasn't painful so much as relieving. As I peeled my skin back, groaning, I felt something push at my rib cage from within. I thought, my god, I must have a tumor between my breasts, now a heart attack is one thing but cancer is just not allowed. And that's when it happened; I don't know how. My heart burst out of my chest. It popped through its arterial fence, it surged through my lungs and my rib cage, and ejected itself through various nervous tissues and muscle fibers with a final rip through the hole I had made in my skin. There it stopped, my heart, still attached to its arteries and veins, but exposed and sagging between my breasts like some kind of unwieldy necklace. Chestlace? If you will.

Because Paul has fucking weird dreams, naturally he assumed this was one and promptly went back to sleep. After a moment, so did I. When I woke up, the problem had not remedied itself. My chest bore a small open wound, from whence my heart dangled, snug between my mammary glands. I was more fascinated than alarmed—fascinated because my heart, now visible to the world, looked remarkably like a tomato, a tomato whose rubbery skin steadily palpitated with soft th-thumps. When Paul woke up, he had an identically similar reaction. Your heart, he exclaimed animatedly, it looks remarkably like a tomato! Then he stopped staring and looked at me concerned. Darling, he said, we really should take you to the hospital, with that patronizing look like he knew what was best, and I certainly didn't. By that point in our relationship, however, I knew better than to cry condescension. He would invariably pull out the card that said, I have a master's degree in women's studies and a four-year background in anti-rape activism. What do you have, Christine?

Fuck you, Paul, I said with a yawn, and got up gracefully. I'm fine. I stepped in front of the mirror to examine myself more closely. Not only did my heart *look* remarkably like a tomato, there was no arguing that it was, in fact, a tomato, and large, at that, even when contracted. Indeed, it took great effort to resist taking a bite out of my heart. I gasped and covered myself, thinking of Paul's similar tomato-lust. I must keep my heart away from Paul, I thought, or he will surely eat it and kill me.

I put on a loose sweatshirt and began to feel somewhat lightheaded. Well, I thought, maybe I'll go to the emergency room after all. I wrote a note and stuck it on the refrigerator, then left the apartment and stepped onto the street. By now I had a severe craving for a big, juicy tomato, so I thought, why not stop at the farmer's market on the way to the hospital. There wasn't any rush.

It was crowded for a Tuesday morning, with everyone tossing around barked numbers and bulky bags of produce. I made my way past tables of green peppers, lettuce, jellies, and cucumbers before catching sight of the tomatoes at the end of the market. Cherry tomatoes, plum tomatoes, slicing tomatoes, ahh. The shiny bright skin, the friendly round shape, the thirst-quenching blood.

Luscious, I thought. Pure lusciousness.

I needed a tomato, right then, right there.

My eyes locked in on an especially large specimen with a quirky asymmetrical stem. This, I thought, this is the one. I felt a twinge of guilt at my independent tomato-hunting. Although Paul and I tried always to prevent any development of co-dependence between us, so much so that we each made our own salads standing side by side at the counter, tomatoes had always been our thing. Now, not a full day since we had made our commitment, I was already acting selfishly. But what can you do about severe tomato cravings, I asked myself, except eat a tomato? Besides, you are selfish.

As I was beelining towards the tomatoes, lost in my thoughts, a woman with an elbow bumped into me. She elbowed me right between my breasts, right in the heart. I sucked in my breath and stopped still. The woman didn't bother to apologize, just stalked off indifferently as my blood went rushing to my head. Had it burst? Had my heart burst? I needed to sit down and check without flashing my breasts at anyone. I needed to sit down and catch my breath.

I sat down. I looked down my shirt. My heart had ruptured; juice was running down my abdomen. I reached down and cradled my broken heart. Realizing I was in a busy public area, I looked up alarmed. No, I calmed myself, no one had noticed me with my hand down my shirt; I had my heart to myself, and rightly so.

Having skipped breakfast, my hunger pangs were intense, and heightened by the smell of ripe tomato. I would need to eat soon. And what more delicious than...? No. I knew better. And yet my stomach was turning itself inside out. So I grabbed my tomato heart and tugged it experimentally towards my lips, finding that its arterial vine had some give. I sucked my heart's juice. And...I couldn't help myself. I bit.

Immediately I felt stronger in the stomach and brain but weaker in the rest of my body. My chest hurt badly; pain shot all through. I mustered up all my strength and walked the two blocks to the hospital. The nurse in the emergency room took one look at me, gave me a clipboard, and said, take a seat. Although the pain was excruciating, I told myself to be patient. Other people needed doctors, too. But I couldn't even fill out the application form; my stomach was yawning noisily. What was I to do? So I lifted up my heart and took another bite. The nurse sighed. Well, now you'll need a transplant. Doctor!

I recovered fully. Paul and I decided to take a break. I feel sure it is a permanent break but have decided the decision is his. He will not be at peace unless he gets the last word and can legitimately justify the break-up on grounds not related to my heart.

I no longer eat tomatoes. When I see them now, I feel a phantom lurch in my chest. My new affair is with grapes. Cold, hard grapes. I like the white kind, the seedless kind, the ones that look like eyeballs. I like to plop a cold, hard seedless grape in my mouth and suck and suck before biting and feeling all the juice squirt out inside of me. Sometimes, I like to peel the skin off before chomping on the fleshy interior. But it's hard to find the time for that. We're all so busy these days.

CIRCE

A NOTE ON THIS PRODUCTION:
Verso and recto should be performed simultaneously.

CIRCE'S CROW DÆMON
Cacaw. Odysseus, Odysseus. Everyone loves Odysseus.
(folds wings over stomach in rocking chair)

Athena, too, foolish girl, is in love with Odysseus. She, who has the work of an army—to make the mortals wiser—is all the time swooning over images of Odysseus in her mind.

Athena should be thinking of war and wisdom, but: Odysseus, Odysseus. Everyone loves Odysseus.

Especially Circe. The witch.

From her stronghold on the island of Aeaea, Circe turns men into swine. Women do not visit her. Therefore it is lonely for Circe, for Circe of the lovely hair. Circe has only servants and man-pigs to amuse her. Man-pigs are amusing—hear their pathetic grunts—but lately Circe has been wanting more. Circe has been wanting a lover, a man of fierce intellect with arms strong as pythons around her chest.

So she waits for such a man. She is, because immortal, eternally patient; she will wait as she must.

CHORUS OF BEAUTIFUL WOMEN
(arching, pouting, squatting, hairtossing)
Odysseus of the wily mind of the shrewdness the
unflappable courage the unmatchable cunning the
immeasurable combination of brain and brawn. Odysseus
who has the gods on his side. Odysseus who has the gods
against him.

ATHENA flies across page with lovelorn expression.

*ODYSSEUS charges forth with spear, muscles flexed
and bulging, broad chest smeared with mud and blood.
ODYSSEUS furrows brow at some impossible puzzle,
chewing on his lower lip with vehemence. ODYSSEUS
urinates from the edge of his ship into the river, his piss-
stream strong and equine, raising clouds of steam.*

Enter CIRCE of the lovely hair. CIRCE curtsies.

*CIRCE invites ODYSSEUS' MEN to dine with her. They are
slovenly, indulgent, do not give her her proper due. CIRCE
smiles wickedly, tosses her lovely hair. She nods at HALF-
NAKED NYMPH-SERVANT, who leaves and returns with
a tray of dessert wine. The MEN drink heartily, wipe their
mouths with their sleeves. CIRCE laughs maniacally.
ODYSSEUS' MEN turn into oinky, distressed pigs.*

*From page left, ODYSSEUS flexes, thinks hard. From above,
HERMES drops bottle of immunity into ODYSSEUS' lap.
ODYSSEUS opens it, chugs.*

The story goes that when Odysseus lands on Aeaea and, with the help of Hermes, resists Circe's unmanning potion, Circe will go ga-ga for the god-like mortal from Greece.

She will bed him until he tires of her, and then give him a helpful hint for his journey.

She will be mature and let him, with a wistful kiss on the cheek, go, go back to Penelope, for she is his True Love For Ever And Ever.

Circe will re-man the unmanned man-pigs to show Odysseus that she is righteous and good, and she will respect his and her own autonomy enough to say goodbye with dignity and grace.

(*DAEMON stands up, faces reader with wings extended and eyes pulsing red.*) Not in this story. Cacaw. In this story Circe is selfish and immature. In this story Circe is childish. In this story Circe turns Odysseus into swine.

BED (raised from page slowly):
Creak.

Curtain down.

Enter CIRCE in CIRCE's enchanted palace. In CIRCE's enchanted palace, sunlight shines always, reflecting off of CIRCE's rich hairwaves and glistening skin. CIRCE has forgotten what she looked like prior to discovering she can modify her appearance with a flick of the wrist, a twist of the tongue. But it is a trap, her beauty. She uses it to trick

ODYSSEUS drinks CIRCE's magic potion; it has no effect. CIRCE gasps. ODYSSEUS lifts sword. CIRCE releases MEN from their spell. MEN, naked MEN all around, but CIRCE gazes only at ODYSSEUS. With a flash of her eyes, CIRCE brings her bed to the page with a slam. CIRCE and O fuck.

ODYSSEUS stands on the edge of the page, looks longingly out.

CIRCE *(gives O a wistful kiss)*: Now go, go back to Penelope, for she is your True Love For Ever and Ever.

CIRCE and ODYSSEUS embrace. CIRCE exits page right, ODYSSEUS page left.

VOICE OF CIRCE
Odysseus is mine. *(laughs maniacally)*

Curtain up.

CHORUS OF BEAUTIFUL WOMEN
(tittering)
She's so bright. She's so clean. I'm telling you, she's everything.

MEN into lusting for her, then uses their slavering to justify turning them to beasts as soon she feels vulnerable in their gaze, as she has done with O's MEN. She is beginning to recognize this pattern as a problem. As her MAN-PIGS squeal with snouts roving in the dirt, regret announces itself in her loins.

CIRCE

(to herself) No more blow hot and cold.

ODYSSEUS

(coming upon CIRCE unnoticed) Stitch in my side. Why did I run?

CIRCE/BELLO/BELLA

(turns at O's voice, points to sty) As they are now, so will you be, wigged, singed, perfume-sprayed, ricepowdered, with smoothshaven armpits.

MAN-PIGS

Oink.

BLOOM

Hungry for liver, love. Button goes bip at sight of liver.

CIRCE

(tosses Ulysses aside) Then I shall get you some liver. *(Exits.)*

It is midnight, and all is dark. Over on page left, ODYSSEUS can see the brightened clouds above the palace and he knows something is up. There is enchantment here, and his MEN have not come back.

CROW
(flying above ODYSSEUS as if to warn him)
Peep, peep. Pe-weep.

ODYSSEUS nods up at CROW, steps from page right to page left.

JAMES JOYCE
Welcome to Nighttown. It is one hundred and twenty pages long. Odysseus, c'est moi. Bloo bloom.

CHORUS OF BEAUTIFUL WOMEN
(swooning) James Joyce of the well-groomed mustache of the handsome eye patch the occasional bowtie. James Joyce of the most greatest literary genius. James Joyce, James Joyce. Everyone loves James Joyce.

JAMES JOYCE
Shrug. Vavavoom.

JAMES JOYCE
One hundred and nineteen more pages. *(sniggers)*

Rope plunks onto page, with HERMES making his way down it. HERMES slides an antidote to CIRCE's charms into ODYSSEUS' hand. O drinks it. HERMES and rope are retracted from scene.

CIRCE

(Entering with tray) Sit, sit. *(places chalice and plate before him)* Drink. And take the form of the brute you most resemble.

As ODYSSEUS drinks, CIRCE is distracted by JAMES JOYCE's smugness.

CIRCE

Thou turnedest me into a joke,

ODYSSEUS

(Drinks. No effect.) The sty I dislike. *(Unsheaths sword.)* Kablaaam!

CIRCE'S enchantment has bounced off Odysseus and turned her NYMPH-SERVANT into a swan. Astonished CIRCE of the lovely hair zaps NYMPH-SERVANT back to nymph form and considers her nemesis with sword swung.

CIRCE

(deciding) Penetrate me not with sword but with! *(snaps fingers; bed crashes back down onto page)*

WOMAN, undoing with sweet pudor her belt of rushrope, offers her all moist yoni to MAN's lingam. MAN yawns, thinks of PENELOPE. Impatient CIRCE cracks whip.

ODYSSEUS

I cannot seem to.

FEMINIST
And I quote, "A FEMINIST: *(Masculinely)*" (481).

JAMES JOYCE
(rubs palms together) I've put in so many enigmas and puzzles that it will keep the professors busy for centuries arguing over what I meant.

across page)
.nd my pigs to whores. *(extends arm)* Abracadab.

JAMES JOYCE
(chasing tail) Arf. Rrrrawwrf. Whimp whimmp.

A FEMINIST
Feminist critique of canonical literature A-plus, yet the use of male-female binary seems dated, victimizing, powerful Circe made weak and dependent on male validation. What gives.

(adjusts glasses, listens hard) Sex-positivity good. A-plus.

SYLVIA PLATH
Did you hear my brain go snap?

TED HUGHES
Polysyllabax.

VOICE OF HERMES
(legs hanging down from Olympus) Do not then resist and refuse the bed of the goddess.

ODYSSEUS
(sighs, gives Circe his full attention) Well?

CIRCE AS TALL BLONDE
CIRCE AS FIERY REDHEAD
CIRCE AS SUICIDE GIRL / SYLVIA PLATH
CIRCE AS PRINCESS LEIA
CIRCE AS HELEN

ODYSSEUS
(another yawn) It has certainly been a long day. *(sleeps)*

CIRCE'S SOLILOQUY
(to mirror)
How can this be?
Am I not a beauty?
He is the only man I want
With great yearning in my cunt
And yet he be
Too fatigued?
What this hur swine thee thine no!
There must be a way I can look to please him.

PERCEPTIVE CIRCE OF THE LOVELY HAIR /
AS MOLLY BLOOM
(shakes ULYSSES awake) Poldy! Oh, Poldy! It has been too long.

They embrace. SYLVIA eyes TED. TED eyes CIRCE. Bell jar crashes down, trapping SYLVIA, who beats her fists against the glass, sticks. JOURNALIST snaps picture. Bell jar lifts.

TED becomes STEPHEN DEDALUS.
SYLVIA becomes MATILDA (A TEENAGE GIRL).

MATILDA (A TEENAGE GIRL)
Oh, Stephen. The gods have brought us together at last. *(dizzy)*

CHORUS OF BEAUTIFUL WOMEN
(posturing) Stephen of the excellent tenor, the narrow chest and philosophical mind. Stephen who flies above the constraints of religion, nationality, and politics in his own development. Stephen who has Art on his side, Stephen who has few against him. Stephen, Stephen. Everyone loves Stephen.

STEPHEN DEDALUS
You have the most beautiful eyes.

MATILDA swoons. They kiss. STEPHEN puts arm around MATILDA, then places hand under her shirt to caress her stomach. MATILDA pulls away.

MATILDA
(he touched my fat stomach, he touched my fat stomach)
Stop! Don't do that!

ULYSSES
(lit up) Exuberant female. Enormously I desiderate your
domination. I am exhausted, abandoned, no more young.
I promise never to disobey.

They embrace. ODYSSEUS falls back to sleep.

CIRCE
What, still? *(pokes him)*

ODYSSEUS
(sputtering) Tis Calypso's fault!

CIRCE AS REAL CIRCE, UGLY CIRCE,
WRATHFUL CIRCE WHO IS CHILDISH
(through gritted teeth) Your bed is made, thou. Henceforth
you are unmanned and mine in earnest, a thing of the
yoke. Swine!

ODYSSEUS
(stretching awake) Your classic curves, beautiful immortal.
I was glad to look on you, to praise you, a thing of beauty,
almost. But I do not want to fuck you.

MATILDA
Are you there, Goddess? It's me, Matilda. Goddess, please
I would feel a lo

MATILDA sees that GODDESS ha

MATILDA
Goddess, no! Not you too

STEPHEN

What? What?

MATILDA

Get out. Get out now. *(Roars fire. STEPHEN, hair singed, leaves. MATILDA watches him fly away, her eyes turning to stone.)*

MATILDA

I hate them I hate them I hate them. There's nothing I can do. Except—

CHORUS OF BEAUTIFUL WOMEN

Sit on your hands, don't do it, sit on your hands, don't do it, sit on your hands.

MATILDA gets up, strolls down the hall to the bathroom, and shuts the door. She runs the sink faucet, bends over the toilet, and sticks the butt-end of her toothbrush down her throat.

No, no. That's not right at all. MATILDA doesn't hurl when STEPHEN leaves her. MATILDA has more dignity.

(on her knees across page)
will you turn Stephen Dedalus into an ugly pig?
better if you did.

other things on her mind.

Die. *(roars fire at ODYSSEUS)*

CIRCE
(extinguishes ODYSSEUS) More complicated.

CIRCE
(to ODYSSEUS) Of beauty, *almost*? *(tears of petulant rage)*
Kablaaam! *(tries to pig him again)*

ODYSSEUS
(hopping around deflecting her spells) Master! Mistress!
Mantamer!

Scene freezes. CIRCE'S CROW DÆMON flops

CIRCE'S
Odysseus's magical defenses will not wear off. Though Circe
making him her plaything for some months. We all know, of
When he gets bored, he'll interfere, command her to release

And poor Penelope sits trapped in her home, surrounded by
armed with weapons and want. Poor Penelope of the aging skin
her Odysseus is, when he will return, and what

Go away. *(flings MATILDA to margins)*

MATILDA
(starving self into oblivion) Are you there, Goddess? Are
you there? Goddess?

down in front of it, gets up, shakes self off.

CROW DÆMON
cannot pig him, she manages to tie him up and detain him,
course, that Zeus is watching, letting Circe play her little game.
Odyssesus from her island. Because she must, she will.

greedy men, slovenly men, selfish, egocentric, impatient men
and graying hair turns weary eyes to the sea and wonders where
divine beings he will charm along his way.

FLOATERS

Written with Leeyanne Moore

Wednesday. Longass day at work, but Wednesdays meant Sal's. Always a good crowd, always got the laughs. Sal's reminded Jason why he loved comedy: the control, the feeling of mastery he got when the audience responded to his every move.

Tonight, though. He didn't know. It had been a shit day, literally. This morning when he went to take a piss, he'd found a mess of oatmeal-colored floaters drifting around in the shit-speckled bowl.

Disgusting.

In the greenroom-cum-broom closet, Jason sat and crossed his legs so his foot wrapped around his calf. Last week he'd threatened to dump Ju-Rin if she started up again with the laxatives. Now he'd have to follow through.

He pulled out his phone and debated. No, he decided, shoving it back into his pocket. He'd do it after the set, when he felt powerful.

Now, he was too anxious. He jiggled his legs, trying to work his nervous energy down to just below stuttering fear.

Enter Kevin and Mike. Jason shifted so his ankle rested on his knee.

Kevin drew first, Mike second. Jason got third.

Jason introduced Kevin, and Kevin stepped up to the mic, did his usual.

Jason stood backstage in the gap between the green curtain and the back door, listening to Kevin introduce Mike. Mike went on. Jason listened with half an ear.

The thing was this. The first time they'd talked, weeks ago, she'd lied to his face. Made him think he was imagining everything.

Then last night he'd found more wrappers in the bathroom trash and a box right in the front of the cabinet—she hadn't bothered hiding them. He'd started off with "Baby, I just want you to be healthy." Long silence. He'd followed that with "I can't be with you, you know, if you're...." Another long silence.

The way she looked at him—like he was slightly pathetic. It made the situation surreal.

Next thing he knew, she'd gotten up off the couch. He could hear her in the bathroom, the crinkling rustling of her throwing out all the packets of laxatives she'd squirreled away. It was that easy, he thought, relieved beyond belief. She came out smiling. He hugged her. She wiggled out of his hug and went to clean the dishes. They watched TV together. It was good.

Then this morning he goes to use the toilet and finds a giant 'fuck you' floater is bobbing in it. Black diarrhea slopped under the rim—he got it on his hands lifting the seat. Jesus.

He shook his head. Focus. Mike was introducing him.

Mike walked off stage and punched him in the shoulder. "They're all yours," he said.

Jason, still jittery, took a deep breath. Then he stepped up to the mic.

"What am I going to do?" he asked. He paced back and forth, mic in his hand. The audience watched him. "Relationships, relationships. What am I going to do?"

"Eat me," Mike called out from backstage.

"Thanks, Mike. I need friends like you like I need a sebaceous cyst." The audience chuckled, and the stage felt a little more like home.

"So here's my problem. I'm thinking of dumping my bulimic girlfriend. In fact, I want an upgrade. What I want is...an anorexic girlfriend."

He paused, twitching with nerves. Then he went for it.

"You—healthy audience people out there—may not realize how aspirational this is for me. There's an enormous difference between a bulimic girlfriend and the anorexic. The anorexic girlfriend is the Mercedes Benz of dysfunction. People look at her: is she going to, you know, die? Or is she a model?" A laugh. A big one. "They just don't know. On the plus side—and this must not be underestimated—the anorexic is the ultimate cheap date. How much does water cost? Go to a fancy place, maybe five bucks. Not bad. And a lot of places you go it's practically free. I know of some restaurants that just give it away.

"My bulimic girlfriend, on the other hand, orders a modest four-course meal and then wants to share mine. 'Share.' As in, attack my plate like Godzilla. I went out for Japanese with my girl once, now a chunk of Japan's missing." A couple laughs.

He made a sad, wise trek in a short circle around the stage, then chuckled. "Everyone pities the girl with the eating disorder. But what about her co-dependent boyfriend? What about me? People, a third-world country now lives in my toilet."

They laughed.

"It's like some war zone in there."

He stopped. Turned. "The floaters, for instance. Remember Battleship, that kid's game? It's like that. They're cruising around, they're bobbing, colliding, sinking. G4 to F8. Kghshhrh! Oh no! You sank my battleship!"

More laughter.

"Up, down. Up, down. I now know what inspired the lava lamp."

He stopped again. "Ever hear of *The Creature from the Black Lagoon*? Classic horror film. I used to obsess over it when I was seven. What is a black lagoon exactly? This kept me awake at night." Hand on waist, willing to sound like a prissy nine year old. "*Where* is this mysterious black lagoon?"

He paused. "It's in my toilet.

"I stumble into the bathroom in the middle of the night, half awake. I lift the lid—" He pushed back three feet. "Whoa. Black water in the bowl. It's like toxic sludge, and the smell..." he pinched his nose and grimaced. "Then this fucking webbed claw comes out of the bowl—oh no!"

He froze in a mock crouch.

"But wait!" He sprang up. "I recognize that rubbery claw. 'Hi, honey.' And my girlfriend lets out a little screechy moan."

He made his face as long as possible, rolling up his eyes while he let forth an unearthly howl. The audience died. "'Don't you look cute in there.'" He moaned a few more times, as if she were responding. It killed.

"And I'm like 'Love you, boo. Don't stay in there too late!'—You've been a great audience, ladies and gentlemen!"

He bowed, then rushed from the stage, barely hearing the applause.

Kevin high-fived him. "Yo. Good show."

"Edgy," Mike said, pushing his chair back onto its back legs. "But can he push it further?"

"I'll push it further," Jason said. "Into your *ass*."

When he got home, she was in bed. He found a covered pot on the stove, lifted the lid. She'd made fishcakes, his favorite. He smiled.

Weeks later, Jason was stepping onto the small stage, holding up his hands at the applause. Mike followed and stood at his side, half a head taller. By sheer accident (i.e., Mike was copying him again) they were both wearing white buttondowns, neckties, and vests. It looked good, kind of professional.

"Okay," Jason said, grabbing the first mic. "We're doing things a little differently this evening. I know some of you are already familiar with my act as Mr. Insensitive, so tonight I'm going to bring out my friend—" He motioned to Mike, who stepped forward and grabbed the second mic. "...who's also grossly insensitive, to help me talk about my dysfunctional relationship. Here we go!"

Mike held out a hand to the audience as if to hush them. "We're going to do an improv scene for you tonight."

Jason was rolling his shoulders, getting into character.

"So the first thing—" Mike went on, "the first thing you need to know is that this is a scene between Jason and his girlfriend. I'm going to play the role of Jason."

Jason walked around the stage behind Mike, shaking himself out with a few slick boxing moves. He stepped up. "I, meanwhile, will be playing the role of a four-foot-tall Korean dumpling." Pause for laughter. "Steamed."

They laughed again. Easy audience. Mike was getting hunch-shouldered and—sweet Jesus—somehow making himself look twenty pounds skinnier.

Jason turned to Mike. "Ready to rumble?"

"Ready," Mike said. Then he stepped forward, doing Jason for the first time.

"The first thing that will happen," said Mike-as-Jason, making nervous gimpy hand gestures (fuck you, Mike), "is I'm going to say: We need to talk."

"Then I'm going to give you a sympathetic look," said Jason playing Ju-Rin. "And say 'okay!'" he used a high voice and cute head tilt and got a few titters. "Oh wait." He ducked his head to the side and pulled out a barrette to push his hair back. The audience loved this.

"I'm going to be surprised—I thought you wouldn't want to talk about your bulimia."

Jason-as-Ju-Rin abruptly changed his demeanor. He glowered and, using a deep, croaky voice like the possessed girl in *The Exorcist*, said, "What are you talking about?" The breathy creepiness of his voice had people in the audience screeching.

Mike started to speak, but whatever he said couldn't be heard over Jason's demon voice. Jason-as-Ju-Rin intoned, "Do not name The Issue Which We Do Not Name, ever. Ever." Jason waited for Mike to open his mouth to interrupt him again. "Ever."

Mike-as-Jason asked, "How am I going to talk about it without talking about it?"

Again with the Exorcist voice: "If you were Korean, you'd know."

"So I'm going to apologize—for, it seems—not being Korean."

"I'm highly sympathetic. Not everyone can be Korean." Jason-as-Ju-Rin smirked.

Mike gave him a look. "I'm going to mistake that smirk for a sexy look," Mike-as-Jason said.

"I'm going to indicate it's a theoretical possibility that I could have sex with you—but *only if*—" Jason-as-Ju-Rin said, producing a slip of paper in his hand with a magician's flourish, "*someone* immediately runs to the drug store and gets the items on this very important list."

"I am immediately going to run this very important errand so that we can have the sex we aren't going to ever have—when I notice that laxatives are first on the list."

"I am going to rejoice in the fact that you are *so* stupid! This will give me a cheery bunny look." Jason doing Ju-Rin's cheery bunny look got a laugh.

"I am unable to handle confronting you when you're wearing the cheery bunny look."

"I know."

"I am—"

"Love you," Jason-as-Ju-Rin interrupted, his voice now high and squeaky.

The audience laughed.

"Okay," Jason said to the audience, becoming himself again. "I think that's all the context you need." He turned to Mike. "Let's do it."

Mike-as-Jason nodded and stepped forward.

"We need to talk. About your bulimia."

There was a torturous silence, Jason-as-Ju-Rin using the time to look up and slowly, slowly raise his eyebrow. As he did this, Mike-as-Jason slowly deflated.

The two sustained the moment, staring at each other until they could hear audience members shifting in their seats.

"Run this errand for me? We'll talk after you get back." Jason-as-Ju-Rin held out a list to Mike-as-Jason.

Mike looked uncertain, reaching for the list, but Jason-as-Ju-Rin pulled the paper back.

"No, no. Nevermind. You don't have to."

"Wait—fine—I'll go," Mike-as-Jason offered.

"No," Jason-as-Ju-Rin quickly responded, and held the scrap of paper further out of reach.

"But I want to," Mike-as-Jason responded, trying to grab the paper.

"Nevermind!"

"Want to!"

Mike finally seized the scrap of paper.

"Thanks, sweetie," said Jason-as-Ju-Rin cheerily.

The two men turned together: "And—scene!"

They bowed repeatedly. The applause was staggering.

At home, the apartment reeked and a covered saucepan was on the stove. Jason cautiously lifted the lid and— look who forgot to clean up her vomit. Thanks, sweetie. Fuck. He poured the puke into the trash can and watched the chunks glop over the wreckage: a drippy carton of Neopolitan ice cream, a jar of peanut butter, a carton of orange juice, and then some. He took out the trash: there goes that paycheck. Inside, he washed the saucepan and lid, then sprayed the kitchen with Lysol.

"I gotta ask, man," Noah blurted. It was three months later, backstage at the Beat. "Don't you feel guilty?"

Jason shrugged, yawned. "Noah, when you haven't had sex in six months, the high sperm count just squeezes the guilt right out of you."

Pause. The guys laughed a beat later.

He checked his watch. "Hey, I gotta, you know, get ready," he said. They left.

He stared himself down in the filmy mirror, then turned away from it. Hard to feel guilty with all the shit she put him through. When every time he told her she had to stop, she looked him in the eye and lied: she *had* stopped. When every time he said the right things—she was beautiful, she didn't need to lose weight, he loved her the way she was—she looked at him like he was some idiot.

"The Diary," he announced, holding the mic with both hands. "She leaves it open on the kitchen table, wide open, obscenely inviting me to invade her private thoughts."

He held the mic up and in a dirty, sexy falsetto breathed, *"Read me, you motherfucker—you know you want to!"*

He put the mic on the stand. "But I don't read it. I'm a nice guy."

He smiled. "This drives her crazy," he said. "I know it does. Because I've found the diary open not once," he held out his fingers, "not twice, not three times—but every fucking day for a month.

"So last time she came home, I said, 'Don't leave this out again or,'" he shook a finger at the audience and sang, "'you'll be sorry.'

"And she did. She left it out again." He let them absorb that information, then hauled out the journal from the back of his pants. "Here it is—let's check out the highlights."

Laughter, clapping. He was nailing the timing. But he was also floating on autopilot. Half his mind was on his set; the other half was watching a woman in the audience as she turned and bent over to grab her purse, the knobs of her spine showing through her thin blouse.

He flipped the pages. "Now, if I wasn't stuck for material tonight, I'd go on *not* reading it—because it drives her batshit."

Remembering Ju-Rin in the walk-in closet, he flinched. Ju-Rin kneeling, bent over a giant Ziploc bag in her fancy dress, her vertebrae pushing through her skin. He'd caught her in the bathroom mirror as he was getting ready for their date last week, dinner at a fancy restaurant to celebrate this very gig. Her fingers went deep; tears leaked out her eyes as her slimy fingers hammered down the back of her throat.

"See, I've *learned* about myself through this relationship. Isn't that nice, to really learn about yourself? I've learned...that I'm one passive aggressive sonofabitch." The audience laughed.

He stared at her in the mirror. Don't bother to close the closet door or anything. Jesus. As if she sensed his stare, she glanced up and met it in the mirror, her eyes wet, defiant, her fingers still going at it, reaching down. Then she shifted so he couldn't see her face, just her back as her head bent down, the hard bolts of her spine jerking above the low-cut back of the dress.

"I've also learned that my passive aggressiveness is on a whole other level from hers. Infinitely more passive, infinitely more aggressive," he said over the laughter.

"So bring it on, *bitch*."

He pulled open the medicine cabinet mirror a little bit more, angled it so he could watch. The rice porridge came up in small spurts of gooey whiteness. Her fingers went back at it with vigor, wetly stroking. He watched them push down deep to trigger her gag reflex. Her jaw muscles worked to widen further until she looked like she might swallow her own hand.

Her fingers left a glistening trail of saliva from her wet lips, and he pressed his boner into the edge of the bathroom counter.

Later, at the restaurant, he'd said to her, "So, when are you coming to see the new set?" The fork paused on the way to her lips. She chewed thoughtfully, then said she didn't want to jinx him. Things were going so well.

"They are, aren't they?" he said. They clinked their glasses.

He frowned down at the page in front of him.

"Okay. June 11th." He cleared his throat. "Things with Jason are going so well...."

The audience roared.

MY FATHER AND I
WERE BENT
GROUNDWARD

KILL MARGUERITE

My father and I were bent groundward and picking up pebbles while arguing in our confused, disconnected way, when from up above and behind us the sword of Hephaestus swung down mercilessly to slice my father all the way plumb from his asshole through to his left hip. Then for a second go it came back around, back into the asshole and down through the groin to sever his left leg completely. The sword of Hephaestus was forged of a bronze and silver hybrid that changed color from bronze to silver to blinding in the light. It was lean and strong, and handled effortlessly as it whipped through my father's ass.

Before disengaging itself from his body, my father's left leg shivered a bit, then plopped over and into the sand. From his pelvis, blood sprayed in an arced line, like water from an oscillating sprinkler. I rushed towards him, sorry for all I had said, and intending to offer support before he lost balance completely. As I ran I saw with horror from the corner of my bulging, terrified eyeball that the sword of Hephaestus was now swinging swift and directly toward me. There was no getting away: I knew this, and flinched. The sword of Hephaestus caught me between the thighs and sliced off my right leg, easy. The blade took an abrupt swerve then, the flat side slapping my ass before striking the ground and rescinding into an overcast sky.

As you might guess, we hopped around screaming as blood gushed out of our hip joints and clotted the sand into crimson lumps. Having always been the more competent in times of crisis, I bent down, wincing at the pain in my sliced socket, and picked up my father's left leg and my right leg, respectively. I ordered my father to walk west along the river. I linked my arm with his and we managed to pogo together, like the elementary school field-day game where you tie your right leg to somebody else's left leg and become a three-legged creature, only we had no third leg to share. All the while, my father wouldn't look at me, not even a sideways glance. I spent the time wondering what Hephaestus had meant by such a mean swipe; he of all the gods seemed most likely to be sympathetic. In silence, we continued to take generous hops by turn, our remaining legs strong as steel, as we advanced towards the closest hospital, where the doctors stitched us back up, saying we were lucky he didn't slice through our hearts.

I guess we weren't supposed to have gone to the hospital, because it made things a lot worse in the long run. A few hours after arriving back home, where my mother stirred spaghetti in a strong steel pot, I felt a strange rumbling in my hip socket precisely where my leg had been stitched back on. My father expressed feeling a similar quake in the middle of his left pelvis. That was when I knew we were to bear immortal children from our wounds. I quickly unlaced my stitches and pulled off my leg, allowing a full-grown god named Meninges to spring out, panting heavily; he had almost suffocated in there. My father did the same with his stitches, and from his pelvis leapt a beautiful goddess named Hysteria, with golden locks, coral lips, and the rest.

Hysteria and Meninges immediately embraced, ignoring their injured parents. My father and I stitched ourselves back up; it's not hard once there are holes to guide you. Looking at one another, we each saw our children's mythologies in the other's face. They would love each other, grow old together, despite/because of having an unusual sex life and an uncommonly high number of shared genes.

It has been difficult knowing my son's father is also my sister's father: it's like in the movie *Chinatown*, with the difference being obvious. For me, this has all been a small if unusually sharp bump in the proverbial road of life; for my father, it has been a wall. He walks now with an imagined limp; his head, shoulders, knees, and toes all drag, increasingly lifeless as the years proceed. But my father has always been a homophobe. The knowledge that his immortal child was born with the sword of another man, and the ugliest of gods to boot, is simply too humiliating. This is what we had been arguing about in the first place: why I was so unfeminine, and couldn't I be normal. I had said I don't like being penetrated. He had claimed to dislike it as well.

We have never much talked about our experience with Hephaestus. It is the elephant in the room, as you can imagine. It's discomfiting to have these scars, like matching tattoos, marking the history of what we most wish we had not been through together. Otherwise we're not very close, which I've always thought a shame. We're alike in so many ways.

TWINS

ELIZABETH'S LAMENT

Told partly through the lyrics of Tegan and Sara

Jessica,

I ask myself all the time how two people who look so precisely the same can be so utterly different and I'm sure that you do too. For instance how we're mirror images with the same shoulder-length, sunstreaked blonde hair, sparkling aquamarine eyes, and perfect golden skin. And then how beneath our skin there is a world of difference. For instance how I'm selfless and caring while you are selfish and cruel. For instance how you live as if you're one while I live as if I'm two, an us, a we. Well today my therapist gave me this book called *The Emotionally Abusive Relationship* and sis, it's us to a tee. According to the book you withhold love and belittle my feelings so I no longer know who I am. Read the pages, Jessica. It's you. The abuser. You.

How can you live so happily while I am sad and broken down? In order for our relationship to work we have to respect one another's strengths and roles in the relationship. Respecting my strengths and roles in the relationship is something you do not do. All you do is what you want to do even when it negatively impacts me which is fucked. Remember that time you sabotaged my carefully planned campaign rally because you don't care that I have feelings? That time you tricked my hunky date into thinking you were me while I waited for hours thinking I got stood up? That time you wanted to date Todd just because I did? All the times you get me to do your dishes or homework just so you'll say you love me the most and we'll get sundaes tomorrow but then when I show up and you've already ordered with Lila. And you're so sorry, it'll never happen again, but it happens the next time too. And when I ask you to stop wearing my new barrette without asking, you say sure but then you keep wearing my new barrette without asking.

The book says you do these things because creating chaos in the relationship gives you a sense of freedom from the stifling confinement of intimacy. I understand. But Jess, when you act like this, when you get so into yourself, I lose sight of common goals and who I am within them. I spend all night losing sleep, sick inside wondering where you're leaving your makeup and then I wake up and see you and it's like I've never had feelings before in my life. Jessica, there's a war inside of me. I hate your guts sometimes but sometimes you're so fun and I don't know how to act because I hate your guts Jessica but sometimes you're so nice to me and I don't know how to act because I hate your guts Jessica but sometimes you really love me and I don't know how to act because I hate your guts I hate them I hate them your guts I hate them Jessica—

The book says for our relationship to work, we have to communicate. What I'm communicating now is this isn't working. You have to change. From now on, you're gonna do your homework yourself and quit being so fun all the time. You're gonna be responsible and I get to be the fun one. I'm gonna forget Dad's birthday and you get to say your present's from both of us. You did get Dad a present, didn't you?

What a surprise. See how you're nothing without me.

I know you're sorry. You're always sorry. "I'm Jessica, and I'm the sorriest twin in the world." I don't want your empty apologies. What I want Jessica is—are you listening?—because listening's not your strong suit so listen. What I want Jessica is your private time. I want you close. I want you to stay home and keep our memories warm with me. I want to spend the evening watching you get yourself clean. I want to shave my head and lie in bed with you all day long. I want you to tell me you love me more each time you look into my eyes. I want you to look me in the heart and promise no love's like our love. Tell me I'm what your hands were made for, I'm what your mouth was made for. Don't you want that too?

You know what, nevermind. I know my screaming and shouting won't keep you. No hissyfits, mind my manners. I won't make your love so scared to come through our yard. Because when it comes down to it, Jess, when we work, we really work. Jess, I really love us. How we look so alike, and yet are different. Like when I'm staring into my own eyes in the mirror and thinking they're yours and you're being so sensitive for once, you're really seeing me, but then I blink and it's just me. Or I'm looking at you and I try to smoothe your eyebrows by smoothing mine, like you're the mirror, you're me, because you are except you're not. And sometimes when I creep into your room and rub my face in your sweaters which are scratchy but soft like you, I know we have more than just twin sense, that special feeling and who am I kidding, I hate myself I'm boring I read too much I wish I were you. But I'm not you. I'm only ever the opposite of you. Even dressing bad is like loving you. There's nothing love can't do.

What was that? I have been imprisoned all my life by an evil double of myself and all you can say is you are who you are? You are who you fucking are. Well. You must not understand relationships because in relationships who you are depends on *the other person*. For instance see what happens when I rip off your purple miniskirt and wear it myself. Do you see how fun I am when you're not around? How I'm carefree and spontaneous. How I wear tighter clothes, I don't have to individuate. What. I'm communicating. What. I'm sick of being Elizabeth all the time, the Elizabeth to your Jessica when I'm the older twin, you duplicate me.

So do it—duplicate me. Now. Move your leg when I move mine. Cross your legs when I cross mine. Stop. You're not doing it right. You're not—you never. Jessica. I'm warning you. Jessica. Jessica. Jessica. Jessica. Jessica. Do I have to kill you. Jessica. Good. We are breaking down the wall between our bedrooms, Jessica. We are breaking down the wall between our bodies. Like O like H in your gut. Our gut. Ours. Are you all right. We can stand up straight. Because no matter what happens between us, I collapse. No matter what happens, you can't escape me, can't untangle. Because I felt you in my life before I ever—collapse.

SWEET VALLEY TWINS #119:

ABDUCTED!

Some language has been appropriated from *Sweet Valley Twins*, numbers 5, 9, 12, 14, and 34, created by Francine Pascal; *Choose Your Own Adventure #3: Space and Beyond* by R.A. Montgomery; *My Teacher Is an Alien* by Bruce Coville; and *The Baby-Sitters Club #35* by Ann M. Martin.

"Lizzie!" You look up to see your twin sister standing on the back porch. "There you are!" she exclaims, spotting you on the lowest branch of the huge pine tree in your backyard. This is your 'thinking seat,' the spot you come to whenever you need to be by yourself and do some serious thinking.

"Time for dinner," she informs you, tossing back her long blond hair. She grins sheepishly. "Will you help me with math after?"

You smile. Looking at Jessica is just like looking into a mirror. You have the same long, blond hair, the same blue-green eyes, even the same dimple in the left cheek. But though you look identical, the two of you are very different.

Lots of people think of you as the serious one. That isn't exactly true—you like having fun with your friends. But you also like having time alone, by yourself, to read, or write, or just think. You hope to become a professional writer some day.

Jessica, on the other hand, never likes being alone. She wants lots of friends around her all the time, and she isn't very interested in anything serious, especially school. Mainly she likes having fun—though her idea of fun sometimes gets her into trouble. And she always counts on you to get her out of it.

The two of you have different friends, different interests, and different personalities. But you are still the best of friends.

"Sure, Jess," you agree. "I'd be happy to."

"Lizzie, you're the best," Jessica beams. "Your turn to set the table!" She vanishes inside.

You get up and follow her, grateful for the distraction. You've been sitting in your 'thinking seat' for quite a while, replaying in your mind the strange encounter you had with your favorite teacher, Mr. Bowman, after school. You can't seem to wrap your head around it. Mr. Bowman supervises *The Sweet Valley Sixers*, the weekly newspaper you founded for the sixth grade. He's a really good teacher, but he dresses terribly. When you stepped into his classroom after school to finish up an article, he was wearing a horrible striped jacket—and speaking in clicks and static into a futuristic handheld device!

Heart thudding, you hid behind the door. Mr. Bowman had been acting odd the last few days, rarely smiling and easily losing his patience. You figured it was stress—student council elections had created a ton of extra work for *The Sixers*. But now it seemed clear that something else was going on. When you finally got up the nerve to sneak a look around the door, you saw Mr. Bowman reach up to his head, grab his ears, and peel off his face!

As he stripped away the mask, you could see he had skin the color of limes. His enormous orange eyes slanted up and away from his nose. A series of muscular-looking ridges stretched from his eyes down to his lipless mouth.

You are Elizabeth Wakefield. And your English teacher is an alien.

Go on to the next page.

After dinner, you head upstairs and start in on your homework unfocused, your thoughts on 'Mr. Bowman's' gruesome face. Within minutes Jessica explodes like a blond bomb in the middle of your history book. "I think I need help from someone who got a four-minute head start in the world!" she sings. The two of you always joke about the fact that you're four minutes older than Jessica. Sometimes you really *feel* like a big sister to your headstrong twin.

"Jess, come on," you sigh. "I'm busy."

"You said you'd help me with math," she reminds you, her blue-green eyes pleading. "We have a test tomorrow and I still don't get long division."

"What do you expect?" You shut your textbook angrily. "You've been copying my homework this entire unit!"

"Lizzie, don't yell." She gives you her most helpless look. "You know I was stressed out when Ms. Wyler explained it. If you'd help me out this one time, I'd never forget it for a trillion years."

"Obsessing about Johnny Buck isn't stress!" you say, referring to your sister's rock star idol. But you can never stay annoyed at your sister for long. "I'm sorry, Jess. It's just—I think Mr. Bowman is an alien."

Her eyes widen. "No way." She sits down on your cream-colored bedspread and listens while you tell her everything: the noises, the device, the mask.

"How awful!" Jessica cries. "What do you think happened to the real Mr. Bowman? What if he's been taken hostage?"

"Poor Mr. Bowman!" you gasp. "What should we do?"

Jessica jumps to her feet. "I have an idea!" Her blue-green eyes light up with inspiration. "If the device is the alien's only connection to his home planet, he'll be stuck here without it. So we'll steal it. Then we can use it as leverage to save Mr. Bowman."

"Good thinking, Jess!" It's moments like these when you admire your twin's scheming mind. "But that sounds dangerous."

"It'll be a piece of cake. Just get someone to distract him during class tomorrow and swipe it when he's not looking."

"I don't know, Jess," you say. "You know how I feel about stealing."

Jessica paces across the room, her sunstreaked blond ponytail bouncing up and down with each step. Suddenly she stops and twirls to face you. "I know!" she exclaims, her aquamarine eyes sparkling with excitement. "Why don't I do it? We can switch identities during first period."

You chew your bottom lip. While Jessica always enjoys secrets and pranks, you dislike doing anything deceptive. "Why can't you just wait until you have English?"

"I'm too suspicious! There's no way Jessica Wakefield can get away with nosing around Mr. Bowman's stuff. But *Elizabeth* Wakefield can get away with anything!" You nod, seeing her logic. "Besides, if we switch during first period, then you can take my test!"

You cross your arms. "No way, Jess," you say firmly. "That's cheating."

"But it would be so simple, Lizzie. And no one will know the difference."

If you agree to switch identities with Jessica tomorrow, turn to page 112.

If you refuse to switch identities with Jessica tomorrow, turn to page 128.

As usual, you find your twin impossible to resist. "I have a feeling I'm making the biggest mistake of my life," you say, relenting. "But okay."

Jessica flashes you a bright smile and hugs you as hard as she can.

The next morning, you dress in the outfit Jessica put together for you: an uncomfortably short electric blue minidress with purple opaque tights. Jessica always makes a point of wearing at least one purple article of clothing. She does this because she's a member of the Unicorn Club, and every girl in the club does the same. The Unicorns are very exclusive, and consider themselves to be as beautiful and special as the mythical animal of the same name.

Soon, with Jessica dressed in the striped sweater and blue jeans you've picked out for her, the two of you are strolling down the tree-lined streets of Sweet Valley, California, a town which both of you think is the most perfect place on earth. As always, the sun is shining in a blue sky that's dotted with only the tiniest puffs of clouds. With weather like this, it's even harder to believe that your school has been infiltrated by an alien.

You part ways with your twin in front of your locker. "Good luck," you say. "And be careful."

"Oh, Lizzie," she smiles. "Don't be such a worrywart!"

You have a bad feeling about this.

Go on to the next page.

As you're walking down the tiled hallway to math class, you hear your twin's name.

It's Lila Fowler, Jessica's best friend. She hurries to catch up with you, tossing her chestnut hair behind her shoulder. "That minidress is fabulous!" she exclaims.

The only daughter of one of the wealthier men in Sweet Valley, Lila is one of the richest and snobbiest girls in school, and you don't like her very much. But you stop and wait, faking a smile.

"Whoa," Lila whispers. "Check out Lois Waller. She can't even fit into sweatpants anymore!"

Although you don't know Lois well, you feel sorry for the pudgy girl. You've noticed that she has clear skin and remarkable facial bone structure. If only she'd lose some weight, she'd be pretty.

Determined not to blow your cover, you search for a catty remark. "What a tub," you say.

Lila laughs appreciatively. "Come on. We'll be late to math." You hurry to Ms. Wyler's classroom. As you enter, Lila leans into you and whispers, "Remember the plan."

Plan? What plan?

You take Jessica's seat in front of Ellen Riteman, who smiles and waves. Lila sits behind her. Ellen is a snob, too—not as rich or as smart as Lila, but just as nasty. Like Jessica, they're both members of the Unicorn Club. Ellen leans forward and whispers, "Don't forget."

You narrow your eyes. What could the 'Snob Squad' be planning now?

"Scoot to the left," she whispers. "I can't see."

You can't believe it. Ellen is planning on copying off 'Jessica,' which means Lila is planning on copying off Ellen. 'The plan' is a web of cheating, and you're caught right in its center!

As Ms. Wyler begins passing out the test, you're fuming. Jessica must have set up this 'plan' after you'd agreed to help her with math and then conveniently 'forgotten' to call if off. You'd like to think she was so caught up in the problem of 'Mr. Bowman' that she did genuinely forget, but you know your twin's self-serving ways too well. How could she put you in this position?

If you deliberately fail Jessica's test, go on to the next page.

If you do your best on the test but block Ellen's view, turn to page 116.

Serves her right, you think, positioning your test by the edge of your desk where Ellen has the best view. You tackle the first division problem, deliberately miscalculating the subtraction. Failing a test is surprisingly hard, you are thinking, when you hear a scream from down the hall.

It's Jessica.

Let her scream. The more you think about being set up as the center of a cheating ring, the angrier you become.

But you hate having these bad feelings about Jessica.

You hear another scream and hit the ground running. You blast into Mr. Bowman's classroom and push past all the sixth graders standing at the window with mouths agape. Outside, hovering above the soccer field, is your sister, caught in a beam of light. Jessica is being transported into a spaceship, caught in the grip of 'Mr. Bowman,' who has revealed to the school his true alien face.

If you call the cops, turn to page 125.

If you climb out the window to save Jessica, turn to page 127.

You are doing your best to block Ellen's view, ignoring the pencil jabs in your back, when you hear a scream from down the hall.

It's Jessica!

You race down the tiled hallway and storm into Mr. Bowman's classroom, where you find Jessica holding the futuristic handheld device and staring at 'Mr. Bowman' with horrified eyes. 'Mr. Bowman' has ripped off his mask and is shrieking mechanically. The classroom erupts in screams.

Through the window, a beam of light has entered the classroom and is beginning to wander around the perimeter.

You grab the device from Jessica. It appears to be some kind of touch-activated transmitter. Now the beam of light is approaching you. You scan the transmitter for an off button and find a small, unobtrusive indentation the size of a thumbprint.

Hmmm.

If you press the indentation, go on to the next page.

If you toss the device at 'Mr. Bowman's' feet, turn to page 118.

Panicked, you press the button. Immediately you find yourself immobilized within a laser beam.

You feel your body being lifted, and watch as Jessica rushes toward you.

"Jess, no...!" you try to yell, but can't move your face.

Grabbing your arm, your twin tries to yank you out of the beam—but instead gets sucked right into it. Now both of you are being transported up and out of the window—and into the flying saucer!

Once inside the spaceship, you are greeted by a small band of aliens similar in appearance to the alien impersonating Mr. Bowman. Their orange eyes fierce and unblinking, they stare at you with an expression you don't understand.

"What do you want from us?" Jessica shouts.

One of the aliens steps forward and speaks in delicate clicks and clacks into another device that must, you assume, be some kind of translator. The alien presses a button, and the device relays in smooth English: "Our kind is in jeopardy. Our planet has been taken over by vice. We need a leader who can direct our citizens to live moral lives. Which one of you is Elizabeth Wakefield of Sweet Valley, California?"

You stare at your twin alarmed. Jessica returns your troubled look.

"What will happen to the one of us who isn't Elizabeth?" you ask boldly. The device translates, and the alien responds.

"We have no interest in the other one."

If you tell them you are Jessica to ensure that your sister can live, turn to page 119.

If you tell them you are Elizabeth but that you will not be separated from Jessica, turn to page 121.

You toss the device at 'Mr. Bowman's' feet. The beam of light freezes, then jerks forward to grab the device and 'Mr. Bowman' with it. He shrieks mechanically as the beam lifts him out of the classroom and transports him into the spaceship. You are still catching your breath when the doors of the spaceship close and the aircraft departs.

Your classmates turn to you with pale, shocked faces.

"Jessica, you saved the day!" Amy Sutton, your best friend, cries.

"I'm Elizabeth!" you say.

"Jessica! Jessica! Jessica!" the class cheers.

No one knows who you are.

The End

"That's Elizabeth," you say, nodding at your sister. "I'm Jessica."

"What are you doing?" Jessica whispers. "They'll separate us!"

The translator erupts in clicks and static. The head alien nods. At this signal, two aliens advance. One seizes Jessica and the other seizes you.

You are discarded in outer space. You float around for a while, wondering where you went wrong. If only you had made different choices...

Go on to the next page.

You have one secret weapon left that you have not used.

If you think the secret weapon is a time travel device, turn to page 122.

If you think it's something else, turn to page 123.

"I'm Elizabeth," you say. "But I can't be Elizabeth without Jessica. I won't help you unless you keep us together."

The translator erupts in clicks and static, and the aliens confer. Finally, one of the green creatures slides another weapon-like device out of hir belt and points it at you and your twin.

You are alone. What happened? Where did...what. You can't remember. But something about you is different.

You smile beatifically at the small group of Xandari astronauts before you. You are ready to shape their world after your image.

You are treated regally on Xandar and soon you have rehabilitated the planet.

One day you are reading in your new 'thinking spot,' a holographic tree modeled after the one in your memory, when your xalamdak, a common Xandari pet, jumps onto your shoulder and starts scratching at the back of your neck. Huh. You've never noticed that lump. You ask a leading scientist to take a look at it. Ze pokes around in your skin and discovers some teeth, some hair... a kind of subcutaneous teratoma, ze says, converting to Human English via translator: what Human Earthlings call a parasitic twin.

That strange feeling returns, the shadow of some forgotten memory wrenching you with guilt, sorrow, unbearable psychic pain. You think of the book you are reading, shove the feeling away. It's a good book.

The scientist extracts the teratoma and places it in a radiation oven to be disintegrated.

The End

Your secret weapon is a time travel device shoved into your hand by one of the aliens before you were discarded in outer space. There appear to be multiple language settings: you revolve the cylinder until it reads EARTHLING – HUMAN – AMERICAN ENGLISH. A digital display asks you to choose a date and time.

If you would like to return to this morning and try again, turn to page 138.

If you would like to return to Sweet Valley a week ago, before any of this happened, turn to page 140.

If there are always more than two choices, turn to page 137.

You might as well test out the gizmo that one of the aliens stuffed into your pocket at the last minute. The device is lightweight and ridged, with three indentations. You slide three fingers into the indentations and hold your breath.

The device spits out a horizontal beam that scans your body. Your atoms bend. Your vision blurs. The next thing you know, you are inside an unfamiliar bedroom surrounded by strange—but human—girls.

Club meetings always start at five-thirty on the dot, as soon as Claudia's digital clock flips over from five twenty-nine. The clock reads five twenty-eight, so you've arrived in plenty of time. You grab Claudia's desk chair and straddle it. Mary Anne and Stacey are perched on the bed next to you, and Kristy is sitting, as usual, in the director's chair, wearing her visor.

Most of Claudia is inside her closet. She's poking her hand into every compartment of her shoe bag. You have an idea of what she might be looking for, and sure enough, when she finally backs out of the closet, she's gripping a bag of M&M's in one hand and a package of Twinkies in the other.

The Baby-sitters Club was all Kristy's idea. That's Kristy Thomas, president of the club. She's always coming up with excellent ideas, but this one has to be the best. It all started at the beginning of seventh grade. Kristy and her brothers would baby-sit for their younger brother David Michael most of the time, but when they couldn't, Mrs. Thomas would have to make a ton of phone calls to try to line up a sitter. One night as her mom was doing this, Kristy had one of her Brilliant Brainstorms. What if parents could reach a whole bunch of experienced sitters with just one call?

And so the BSC was born.

Besides being brilliant, Kristy can also be bossy at times. She's small for her age and is kind of a tomboy. She wears the same thing every day: jeans, a turtleneck, a sweater, and running shoes. Mary Anne Spier, the club secretary, has brown hair and brown eyes, just like Kristy. But while Kristy is loudmouthed and always in the spotlight, Mary Anne is extremely shy and sensitive. She and Kristy are best friends, but they are so different that you sometimes wonder why.

Claudia Kishi is the vice-president of the club and is, well...*gorgeous*. She's Japanese-American and has L-O-N-G silky black hair, a perfect complexion (despite her incurable junk-food habit), and almond-shaped eyes. Claudia's best friend is Stacey McGill—together they're the most sophisticated dressers in all of Stoneybrook. Stacey is from New York, and Claudia's an artist.

And you? You're the alternate officer, which means that you can fill in for any of the other officers if they can't make it to a meeting. You moved here from California when your parents got a divorce. Your first year in Stoneybrook was kind of rough. But you're close to your mom, and you love the house you live in—it was built in 1795 and it has a secret passage and maybe even a real ghost. Honest.

If you stay here, turn to page 130.

If you want to test out your secret weapon again, turn to page 120.

You race to Principal Davis's office to call the police. In a few moments you hear sirens! A bullhorn! Authoritative commands! Three officers have arrived on the scene. You rush to them but are rudely brushed off.

"Elizabeth Wakefield has been abducted by aliens," goes the rumor spreading through the tiled hallways as students and teachers spill out of classrooms to watch the spaceship vanish into the sky. But you're Elizabeth Wakefield, you try to tell them. No one will listen.

The police officers take out cylinders resembling spray paint cans and speak into them. They start spraying the whole school, and, eventually, the whole world, with forget-Elizabeth-Wakefield-and-what-happened-with-the-aliens mist. Immediately, you forget what you are doing and who you are. You know that something is wrong—you have the distinct feeling that you are not who you say you are. People keep calling you Jessica. You're not Jessica. But who are you?

A snobby girl named Lila claims to be your best friend. She walks you home, where you recognize your parents and brother, Stephen. In your sunny, Spanish-tiled kitchen, the fifth chair at the dinner table sits vacant, but no one mentions it. There's a fourth bedroom that appears to be someone else's, but no one questions it. It must be for guests, you assume, and occasionally sneak in to steal clothes that conveniently fit you. All of the double sets of items in the bathroom are just extra, you decide, because when someone really needs something, she should purchase two sets, just in case. You live according to this rule throughout your life.

Still, something in your soul feels empty, incomplete. Years of therapy are useless, and you learn to live with the feeling of non-identity.

A decade passes. One day, a thirteen-year-old girl shows up at your door claiming to be you. Indeed, she reminds you of you. The similarities are striking. She calls you Elizabeth, but you have no idea what she's talking about. You're Jessica. Who's Elizabeth? She is institutionalized. You think of her from time to time, but can make no sense of the situation. Eventually, you forget the whole thing.

The End

If only you hadn't hesitated—you might have saved Jessica!

"Take me!" you scream, and hurtle through the second-floor window after them. You drop into the bushes and hit the ground running. "Take me!" you scream again, shaking with terror and remorse.

"Don't worry," laughs 'Mr. Bowman,' his metallic screech grating on your ears. "You're coming, too." He pulls out a laser gun and aims it at you. A thick beam of light engulfs your body and pulls you toward the beam that is transporting Jessica and 'Mr. Bowman' into the spaceship.

Once you and your twin are together in the force field, a strange thing happens. You begin to merge. Your bodies suction themselves together. It's as though you are swallowing each other whole.

You have been waiting for this your entire life.

You_2 are treated regally on Planet Xandar. You_2 decide this planet is a good planet and that You_2 will not return to Earth.

The End

"Sorry, Jess," you shake your head adamantly. "Not this time. I'll steal the device myself."

The next morning, you dress in jeans and a striped sweater and head down to breakfast. When you enter the sunny, Spanish-tiled kitchen, you see your mother standing in front of the stove, making scrambled eggs. Your older brother, Steven, has already wolfed down his meal. He has a couple of textbooks tucked under one arm and is heading for the door.

"Did you have enough to eat?" Mrs. Wakefield asks him. Steven's hearty appetite is a family joke.

As you're eating, Jessica waltzes into the kitchen wearing a short electric blue minidress with purple opaque tights. Jessica always makes a point of wearing at least one purple article of clothing. She does this because she's a member of the Unicorn Club, an exclusive group of girls who consider themselves as unique as the mythical animal of the same name. You, on the other hand, scorn the Unicorns. You think the club's sole purpose is to talk about clothes and boys and to gossip about girls who aren't Unicorns.

Soon you and your twin are strolling down the tree-lined streets of Sweet Valley, California, a town which both of you think is the most perfect place on earth. As always, the sun is shining in a blue sky that's dotted with only the tiniest puffs of clouds, making it that much harder to believe your school has been infiltrated by an alien.

You part ways with your twin in front of your locker. "There's still time," she says hopefully. "Sure you don't want to switch?"

"I'm sure," you say firmly. "Good luck with your test."

Jessica pouts and heads down the hallway to Ms. Wyler's classroom.

You take a deep breath and try to calm yourself. You have a bad feeling about this.

Turn to page 131.

This new dimension is peaceful and good, and its people are friendly and eager to welcome you. No one is in a hurry, and baby-sitting is pleasant. There are no enemies. It's a fine world.

The End

"Elizabeth!"

You turn to see Amy Sutton approaching with a smile. Gangly and thin, with straight blond hair and pale blue eyes, Amy is your best friend. She is also a valuable member of *The Sweet Valley Sixers*' staff.

"What's wrong?" Amy asks. Her expression has changed to concern. "You look upset."

"Amy...I'm going to tell you something awful and you have to promise not to tell anyone. Okay?"

Amy nods anxiously.

As you tell Amy about your strange encounter yesterday, her jaw drops.

"That's terrible!" she says.

"I know," you say. "You and Jess are the only ones I've told."

Always grateful when you demonstrate intimacy with her on par with your intimacy with Jessica, Amy offers to distract 'Mr. Bowman' while you look around his classroom for the device.

Together, you walk to your English classroom.

Go on to the next page.

You take your seat while the other students mill around. 'Mr. Bowman' is writing the homework assignment on the board. You glare. Knowing that this is not a real homework assignment but an alien one fortifies your resolve. You glance at Amy. She nods and approaches him.

Before he follows Amy into the hallway, 'Mr. Bowman' gives the classroom a sweeping glance. You feel his eyes rest on yours for an uncomfortably long moment and sense a malicious alien intelligence beating behind them.

Once he's gone, there's no time to lose. Amid the chatter and activity of the classroom, no one notices when you rush up to 'Mr. Bowman's' desk and open the top drawer, where, you saw, he left the device yesterday afternoon.

It's not there. You check the rest of the drawers. Nothing but paper clips, student essays and—what's this? Your breath catches. Beneath all of the teacherly 'props,' you've uncovered the truth: a file with your name on it. You glance through the doorway and see Amy desperately gesticulating while keeping an eye on you.

You open the file and stifle a cry. Inside are a series of grainy surveillance photographs of you: at your desk, at your locker, eating lunch with Amy and Brooke Dennis.

You've got to find that device!

You drop the file and quickly search the rest of the desk. Nothing. But wait—there's 'Mr. Bowman's' satchel stuffed under the desk. You pull it out and there, inconspicuous next to a thermos, it is: slim and black and shiny, its several lights blinking on and off like eyes.

When you pull it from the bag, it erupts in clicks and static. Oh, no! You hurry to find an off button and see only a small, unobtrusive indentation the size of a thumbprint.

There's a metallic shriek at the door. You look up to see 'Mr. Bowman' rushing towards you. You freeze.

If you press the indentation, turn to page 117.

If you drop the device and climb out the window, go on to the next page.

You drop the device and climb out the window. Before you drop down, you glance back inside. 'Mr. Bowman' is rushing after you; behind him, your twin is racing to your rescue.

"Jess, don't!" you yell. "Stop!" You drop to the ground and start running, hoping against hope that your twin heeds your command.

You are almost past the soccer bleachers when you hear a sizzling sound above and behind you. You look back. A beam of light is trailing you. Soon you are engulfed.

You are transported into a spaceship. Once inside, you are greeted by a small band of aliens who resemble the creature impersonating Mr. Bowman. You are grateful at least that your twin is safe.

One of the aliens steps forward and speaks in delicate clicks and clacks into a mechanical device that is apparently some kind of translator. When the alien presses a button, the device speaks back in smooth English: "Elizabeth Wakefield, our kind is in jeopardy. Our planet has been taken over by vice. We need a leader whose unswerving sense of virtue will direct our citizens to live moral lives. We have been monitoring your behavior for some time now, Elizabeth Wakefield, and have chosen you for this assignment. Now it is you who must make a choice. Willingly be our leader or be cast off into outer space."

If you agree to be their leader, go on to the next page.
If you refuse, turn to page 136.

You straighten your posture. You're responsible, efficient, well-liked. You're a perfect fit.

Your training begins immediately. You learn to communicate in clicks and static. You learn the geography, topography, history, and culture of Planet Xandar, your new home.

Upon landing, your hosts guide you across the planet ceremoniously. Wherever you go, Xandaris are fighting. They want more land, or water, or power, or maybe just excitement. You become their natural leader, because the forces you join are leaderless and tired of conflict.

This is the role you have been preparing for your entire life.

The End

You are discarded, left to float around in outer space and wonder where you went wrong. If only you had made different choices...

In the distance you see another being floating. Could it be...Mr. Bowman! You wave excitedly; he waves back. But you cannot control your movement, and your gesture propels you further away from him. Soon your favorite teacher is out of sight.

You have one secret weapon left that you have not used.

If you think the secret weapon is a time travel device, turn to page 122.

If you think it's something else, turn to page 123.

You're wrong. There are only two choices.
Return to page 122.

Time travel is frightening. Rushing back in time is like riding a roller coaster backward, only faster. You can watch the universe through your private porthole. You see stars born and see them die, you see planets spin off into space, comets come and go, supernovas explode, and all the while you are not even there. You are nothing but pure energy until you pop back into being and time in the tiled hallway of Sweet Valley Middle School.

You race to Mr. Bowman's classroom and burst through the door to stop your twin—but it is too late. Jessica—or is that you?—is holding the futuristic handheld device and screaming as a beam of light enters the room.

"Jessica, no!" you shriek. Your twin looks at you and freezes.

"Jessica, no!"

"Jessica, no!"

"Jessica, no!"

You turn around.

One by one, copies of you are popping into being and time in the tiled hallway of Sweet Valley Middle School. One by one, you are pouring into Mr. Bowman's classroom. Soon the classroom is full of twins.

You stare at one another in confusion.

Jessica screams again—'Mr. Bowman' is inching towards her with a maniacal glint in his enormous orange eyes. You spring into action. You make for the device while other yous rush to pull Jessica to safety. Some of you work to get everyone out of the classroom. The rest of you focus on pulverizing 'Mr. Bowman' with high kicks and punches until he disintegrates into thin air. Your collaboration is seamless. It's as though you are thinking with one mind.

Unfortunately, when you grabbed the device from Jessica's hand, you accidentally pressed some button. Now all of the other teachers are rushing into the room, pulling off their masks to reveal their gruesome true selves. Ms. Wyler, Mr. Davis, Mr. Gavin—all of your teachers are aliens!

The beam of light approaches you. It's searching for the transmitter, you realize, and you throw the device at the group of screeching aliens. The beam seizes them, then retracts, pulling them through the window and into the spaceship. The spaceship vanishes.

You cheer as one.

But you continue to proliferate. There is no end to the Elizabeths popping back into the present from the future. Soon the classroom, the school, the world, is overtaken by Elizabeths.

It is too much Elizabeth. There is not enough Jessica. Eventually you turn on yourself. But you just keep coming.

The End

"There you are, Lizzie!" Your twin leaves the group of boys and girls standing outside the gym and runs toward you. "I've been waiting for ages." You study your sister. Jessica's blue-green eyes are larger than ever, and she looks the picture of innocence. "I've been waiting for ages, too," you retort. You don't understand how Jessica can think of nothing but having fun all the time. But you can never stay mad at your sister for long. Staring at Jessica's excited face is almost like looking into a mirror. Both of you have long, silky blond hair, sparkling blue-green eyes, and dimples in your left cheeks. But even though you look identical, your personalities are very different. You are the more serious twin. You love school, especially English, and hope to be a writer someday. You helped found the sixth-grade newspaper, *The Sweet Valley Sixers*, and spend a lot of your free time writing articles for it. Jessica's favorite activity is talking about clothes and boys. You're used to having disagreements with your twin. From your long, sun-streaked blond hair and sparkling blue-green eyes to the tiny dimples on your left cheeks, it's almost impossible to tell you apart. But when it comes to your taste in friends, clothes, and hobbies, you really are quite different. You are the more serious one. You love school, especially English, and spend a lot of your free time reading and writing. Jessica's favorite activities are shopping and gossiping with her friends, the Unicorns, a group of shallow, superficial girls whom you openly scorn. But in spite of your differences, you and Jessica are still best friends. You always have the most fun when you are together, and tonight is no exception. You can't help giggling at your sister's enthusiasm. Looking at Jessica is almost like seeing double. Both of you have blond, silky hair, sparkling blue-green eyes, and a dimple in your left cheek. But your family and friends know that's where the similarities end. Lots of people think of you as the serious one. That isn't exactly true—you like having fun with your friends. But you also like having time alone, by yourself, to read, or write, or just think. You hope to become a real writer some day. Jessica, on the other hand, never likes being alone. She wants lots of friends around her all the time, and she isn't very interested in anything serious, especially school. The two of you have different friends, different interests, and different personalities. But you are still the best of friends. You open the door and glance at your neat blue-and-cream bedroom with a smile. It wasn't long ago that you and Jessica shared a room and constantly got into arguments. But all that changed once you each had a room of your own. When you and Jessica entered sixth grade, your interests began taking separate paths. But though you've grown in separate directions, there is still no one in the world closer to you than Jessica, and you know Jessica feels the same way. You drop your book on the counter of your bright, Spanish-tiled kitchen and pour yourself a glass of milk. You sigh and throw up your hands. But you can never stay annoyed at your sister for long. Being twins makes you as close as any two people can be. From your long blond hair to the dimples in your left cheeks, you are exact doubles in appearance. But that's where the similarities end. Jessica likes to spend time with her friends, gossiping and talking about clothes. You enjoy time with your friends, too, but you also like time to yourself for reading and thinking. Despite your differences, you will always be best friends. Together you stroll down the tree-lined streets of Sweet Valley, California, a town which you think is the most perfect place on earth. You think Sweet Valley is the most perfect place in the world. There is no spot on earth so perfect as Sweet Valley.

You seem to be experiencing some kind of glitch.

The End

INCEST DREAM
OR
SLAM POEM FOR E

I had sex with my cousin. It was a dream.

I had sex with my cousin, who is from a different walk. She is in the proverbial mud, while I am two floors up with three degrees and cats with special diets. We are both poor.

I had sex with my cousin, who is black; I'm white. Or she's biracial, but identifies as black, or has Gone Over to the Dark Side, as my mother has said. My mother says the same thing about me, substituting Other for Dark, because I'm a dyke, and discomfiting. I am not, actually, poor.

I had sex with my cousin, who is fat. She has three kids by different fathers. She is in and out of jail, of rehab. She stutters. Her mom is mean. Her nose is always running. We're the same age, born the same year, slept in the same bed at our grandmother's house when we visited as kids. My middle name is her first name. She was and is a heavy breather. We are the only girls of eleven cousins, thirteen if you count our uncle's two adopted sons from El Salvador but we don't because our parents don't.

I had sex with my cousin. We're talking father's side of the family. My cousin's mom, who's my father's sister and my aunt, is a manager at Wal-Mart and a seasonal school bus driver. My cousin's father left before or after she was born. I can't say if my aunt expected him to stay. I can't say if child support has been arranged or given. One of my cousin's mom's three brothers, my cousin's uncle, my father, earns six figures with a government job. Another of her brothers, my and my cousin's uncle, is a business consultant millionaire. The third of her brothers, my and my cousin's other uncle, who adopted the two refugees from El Salvador, lives quietly on a small smelly farm from which he sells chickens and eggs. Possibly he's gay. Possibly my cousin's mom is also gay. My cousin's possibly gay mom and our possibly gay uncle are the black sheep of the family. They're both fat. The millionaire uncle is also fat; nobody calls him that.

I had sex with my cousin, who has stolen checks from my grandmother and made them out to herself to support her drug habit, I guess. This interpretation comes from my mother who gets it partially from my grandmother, my mother's mother-in-law. My father, whose family it is, can't be bothered to call.

I had sex with my cousin, whose first kid, whose name my parents make fun of, idolizes me because I was able to give him undivided attention once for a few hours when he was four. I'm told he's been asking about me ever since, which I understand could lead someone like my cousin, or her mom, who's my cousin's son's primary caregiver, to pretty deeply resent me.

I had sex with my cousin whose mom, my aunt, is kind of butch, and my mother suspects that growing up in a sexist family full of catered-to men made my aunt Want To Be a *Guy*, and I wonder if this is her theory about me, and I wonder if this theory could be partially right, and I wonder so what if it is, when I'm having better sex than she is.

When I had sex with my cousin it had been years since we'd last seen each other, a few Christmases ago, and she'd had her new baby with her, a daughter whose name my parents have not bothered learning. I had been having a stilted conversation with her about her shit job at a gas station when my millionaire uncle interrupted to ask me about graduate school. I turned from her to him like a dog smelling power and so enabled an insipid conversation that spread to the whole room. Nobody asked my cousin anything. Nobody asked my aunt anything. Nobody asked my probably gay uncle anything, except to be mean ("I take it you're eating well?").

When I had sex with my cousin, it was shortly after learning that she'd been pulled over for driving without a license, or for some crime that had to do with driving that led to her being penalized for also driving without a license. Because she didn't have a license, she didn't show them her license. When the cops asked for her name, she gave them mine. I mean, she told them she was me—she used my name. When the cops searched that name and saw the smiling face of a dykey-looking white girl with Illinois residency, the jig was up. The cops maybe called her mom, who maybe called our grandmother, who must have called my mom, who called me to let me know. Or else she was charged with something, which included her being charged with giving a false name, and she had to explain this to her mom, who told my grandmother so my grandmother could tell my mom who could tell me, in case it ever showed up on my record. Because otherwise why would I know, since her mom and my mom have no reason to speak except after Thanksgiving dinner if they're both there and because they're The Women and my grandmother's old, they are charged with the dishes and so do them together, and I have not once offered to help, not wanting to participate in such offensive gendering even though I equally hate the idea of two women doing everyone's dishes, everyone being mostly men. This side of my family is overgrown with men. Tall, heavy men who interrupt you when you talk and share a largeness of cranium that I've inherited. I'll also inherit their jowls.

I had sex with my cousin and as I explored her body with mine, I apologized for getting everything before her, the Walkman, the CD player, the second Boyz II Men album. I had sex with my cousin and as I probed her cunt with my fingers, I told her I hate them all too, how they treat people, how they dismiss and disparage their own family. I had sex with my cousin and while sliding two fingers inside her, I told her she can't hate me, I'm not like them, I can't be, I am not this person sitting silent and well dressed in a stuffy room making little to no effort to play with her kids. I had sex with my cousin and taking a moment from sucking her clit I told her hey, guess what, she is doing okay, she is doing just fine, her children are beautiful and so is she. I don't remember if she responded. I had sex with my cousin and as I shoved into her harder and fuller and faster and deeper until I lost all sense of my hand, I told her I'm sorry, I'm sorry, I'm sorry. Then I woke up.

EARL AND ED

with images by Marian Runk

There once was an orchid named Ed. He fell in total love with a wasp named Earl, who loved Ed back, totally. Together they became something else, not Earl and not Ed but Earl&Ed, wherein there ceased entirely to be Earl or Ed separately, although Earl&Ed retained the specificities of both its components.

Earl + Ed → Earl&Ed.
Earl&Ed ≠ Earl + Ed.
i.e., Earl&Ed > Earl + Ed.
i.e., Earl&Ed = (Earl→Ed) + (Ed→Earl).*

*where → is a form of becoming.

*

Earl&Ed started off as any other insect-flower pair, each being one of many partners for the other. Earl&Ed met in the full bloom of Ed's second spring and Earl's first and only. Ed was opening himself up for any number of interested insects who relied on nectar to survive, while Earl was slurping the nectar of any number of flowers, meanwhile collecting and depositing pollen to contribute to her partners' reproductive cycles. Though this kind of partner-sharing was performed with both duty and respect, neither of them had any special feelings for their partners.

Earl was a wasp. She inhabited a nest made of wood pulp that bulged obscenely from the end of a hollowed-out log. Earl was a worker wasp. Cordial and friendly to her fellow workers, she bzzzzed as she worked, chewing wood into pulp and dutifully facilitating the expansion of the nest. Earl's bzzz expressed the appropriate contentment towards and resignation to her role in the wasp community, which required also that she defend the nest and provide nourishment to its larvae by paralyzing insects and tearing them apart to transport back to her wards.

Earl, a worker, could only ever be leaving to feed and find nourishment for the larvae.

While Earl had spent many days and nights certain that her life and role were decent and worthwhile, increasingly she had been beginning to doubt this. Having again and again watched the male drones around her leave the nest forever to mate with ceremony and adventure, Earl was beginning to recognize the limits of her own life and role.

Earl, a worker, could only ever be leaving to feed and find nourishment for the larvae. She was always having to be returning to chew more wood into pulp. She would be leaving and returning and leaving and returning always and always until her death.

One day Earl was off on a fly, venturing farther from her nest than usual. She flew and she flew, absorbedly contemplating her fixed place in the wasp community and in the ecosystem at large. When she looked into the future, all she could see was work, and small talk, and sameness, until she died when the weather turned. Pah, Earl was spitting in helplessness and disgust, her mouth still gummy with wood pulp, when a great and impossible yearning came upon her. She had caught the whiff of nectar rushing towards her in the wind.

Past the anthills and past their ants and past the sewers and their mosquitoes and past the azaleas and dandelions, Earl feverishly followed this scent to its origin in a decadent orchid whose showy petals and pert sepals fluttered invitingly in the breeze.

Earl stopped short. Earl being intimidated and Earl feeling suddenly and uncharacteristically shy but Earl fervently desiring this nectar, Earl hid on a bush leaf to think.

*

Ed was an orchid. His roots kept him close to the earth. Uncommonly isolated by a fence of stony shrubs, Ed had only grass, and dirt, and earthworms to keep him regular company; the occasional lost ant. With the exception of Anyx the Butterfly, Ed's one long-term partner who would check in on him now and again, most of Ed's winged visitors came upon him by accident, attracted by a whiff of his scent or simply taking the long route back to their homes. Ed's visitors, infrequent though they were, brought him any important news of his community, so that if Ed may have been lonely, Ed may not have understood that he was lonely. Ed was content with his meager and easy slice of perennial life, and in an effort to occupy himself kept up a pronounced interest in understanding weather patterns.

And when Earl landed on Ed's sticky labellum she immediately began thrusting into it.

Ed having heard Earl's bzzzz from the east had turned to face the incoming insect. He hadn't had a visitor all day; his nectar felt swollen in his spur. He rushed to straighten his stalk and fluff up his petals, thereby releasing another whiff into the air.

Earl on his leaf breathing this new scent swiftly sprang forward with lust. Ed regarded his guest curiously. At the sight of Earl's firm body and large and penetrating multiple eyes, Ed's stamen trembled. And when Earl landed on Ed's sticky labellum she found herself so overwhelmed by Ed's scent and shape she immediately began thrusting into it. Although Ed might typically have felt violated by such an act without introductions, this wasp felt good and right on his labellum.

Earl finally controlling and restraining herself crept over to the edge of Ed's right petal. I Like You, she whispered, peering intently into Ed's center.

Ed blushed and hid his face. I Like You Too! he squeaked boldly.

Earl drew out her proboscis and slowly, tenderly sucked up Ed's nectar. Ed shivered with pleasure.

Earl returned to her nest with vigor.

I Like You, she whispered, peering intently into Ed's center. Earl drew out her proboscis and slowly, tenderly sucked up Ed's nectar.

*

Over time as Earl swooped in more and more on Ed and Ed opened up more and more for Earl, between them grew a certain interdependence. Earl being practical and affectionate, and Ed being sensitive and affection-starved, they quickly found that each was the other's complement.

Ed with his impeccable style and elegant posture would arrange his petals strikingly, and Earl would admire his attention to detail. Earl might give Ed an important weather report, and Ed might pass on any gossip brought in from other insects, for instance There Will Be A Fire Drill In The Nest Today, or The Honeybees Lacking Resources Are Plotting To Take Over Your Nest. They would then grow bashful and silent as they conducted the intimate transaction that was Earl's feeding, lingering longer than necessary each time.

Because of their conversational and physical exchanges and their growing ease and delight with one another, Earl and Ed began to look forward to seeing each other more than they looked forward to seeing any of their other partners. Each found this curious and startling, with each avoiding addressing it for fear that in the talking the feeling might fall away.

Then one day Earl swooped in on Ed and found Ed shriveled up and miserable.

Ed, What's Wrong? Earl asked with concern.

Ed shuddered, and Earl understood that something terrible had happened. She hovered anxiously by Ed's side and waited for him to speak.

Ed broke down and sobbed.

Earl not knowing what to do, for this was a new kind of emotional reaction from Ed that Earl had not yet seen, attempted to soothe Ed by telling him calmly about her day. When eventually Ed relaxed, Earl hovered closer.

Ed, I'm Sorry You Feel Bad. Can I Give You a Hug?

Ed nodded, sniffing. Earl vibrated Ed's petals with her body.

There, There, said Earl. Is There Anything You Want To Tell Me?

Ed nodding again breathed deep until he was capable of relating the following information:

Violet the Furry Moth had come in the night and forced her way onto Ed's labellum.

Ed sagged against Earl as he said this. Earl frowned. Stroking his petals gently she murmured Shh Shh.

Earl stayed with Ed that day, and the next and the next. When Ed was feeling better and more secure in his body and world Earl went off on a fly to find and paralyze Violet the Furry Moth with her stinger. She chewed Violet into pieces and then she carried the pieces to the nest, where she fed them one by one to her larvae wards who were jiggling in hungry anticipation.

Earl chewed Violet the Furry Moth into pieces and carried the pieces back to the nest, where she fed them one by one to her larvae wards.

*

The problem was that both Earl and Ed wanted desperately to be exclusive but didn't know how, because the insect-flower community did not support such relationships. Neither wasps nor orchids were considered exclusive by nature, and those couples who did choose such a path were treated as selfish and abnormal freaks who would orchestrate the downfall of their community by preventing orchids from reproducing and wasps from sustaining their nests. But Earl and Ed didn't care.

And so they chose to be in an exclusive and monogamous relationship, regardless of the certainty of their shunning.

*

Naturally the problem was that Earl&Ed was, as expected, shunned. Dromedus the Drone showed up one day to inform them that Earl had been excommunicated from the nest. He did his best to shame her, claiming that her larvae had starved and that the queen her mother would never forgive her, not in a million days.

Earl giddy with love registered little of this, bzzzing over Dromedus in her continued and overwhelming joy. Dromedus leaving in disgust yelled finally, What You Are Doing Is Unnatural. Earl&Ed cuddling with contentment did not even deign to respond.

Word spreading, so began several hours of winged insects swooping by and spitting on them. Earl's co-workers flung wood pulp on Ed's petals and hurled insults and anger at Earl. Traitor. Flowerfucker. Pervert. Protected within Ed's strong petals, Earl&Ed quivered with anxiety, whimpering at every lash of pulp against Ed's body. Earl&Ed pulled themself through the assault with assertions of shared fortitude.

Then the sky broke open and lightning struck. The wasps retreated, grumbling with annoyance. The rain though hard cleared the pulp from Ed's body and cooled his stinging petals.

Earl&Ed had survived.

Meanwhile in the whorl of a nearby tree trunk Anyx the Butterfly had been watching Earl&Ed cuddle in the warm summer rain. Ed's only long-term partner, Anyx had been saddened to learn that Ed's nectar was no longer available to him. But Anyx though disappointed supported Ed's choices, and watching from afar was beginning to understand why Ed had done what he'd done, and even felt a shade of longing himself. He shoved it aside and, when the rain passed, left to find another flower.

*

The problem was that sometimes Earl&Ed would need to split open or apart and return to being Earl and Ed separately. Although this was uncomfortable for all three of the involved entities, it was necessary for continuing to live.

The problem was that Earl was mobile, and Ed was immobile. It was always only Earl who could initiate a splitting of their entity and take off, a lone wasp in the night.

Naturally what the problem was, was that whenever Earl left, Ed couldn't also leave. Earl always came back, but how could Ed be sure of Earl? All he could do was wait, wavering dejectedly in the wind.

Ed had anxiety problems, Earl would say when she returned. Ed needed to trust her and stop being such a worrywart. Ed needed to know that Earl loved him more than anything in this bright big ecosystem and oh, Ed, Earl needed him so much.

But Earl, Ed would reply, What Might Happen To You In The Bad Rain And Thunder? Your Wings Might Get Torn Off. You Might Get Blown Into A Windshield. All Sorts Of Bad Things Might Happen, And I Wouldn't Ever Have Any Way of Knowing!

Earl could say nothing to comfort Ed.

And then Ed, always already fearing Earl's immanent departure, always already convinced that Earl would begin feeding from other flowers if she wasn't already, would be compelled to produce more and more nectar for Earl to take. And Earl would keep taking and taking it.

Ed became the giver. He gave and gave, producing unparalleled amounts of nectar to keep Earl from leaving.

Earl became the taker. She took and took, feeding on Ed's nectar and unable to help Ed cross-pollinate.

Ed gave and gave, and gave and gave, and he gave and he gave until he forgot who he was. He wasn't anybody. He was some small part of Earl&Ed. Who was Ed when there was no Ed, but only Earl&Ed? The Ed who no longer existed apart from Earl&Ed felt bad, and selfless, and used.

On the other side of things was Earl. Earl took and took, and took and took, and she took and she took until she was fat with Ed's giving, and bloated and uncomfortable, like she needed to go for a fly. And so Earl would have to leave. She could only take so much. Earl would feel misused, as though Ed was manipulating her with nourishment into love.

This cycle continued for some time.

Until Earl one day returning from an unusually long fly looked at Ed, took a long and hard and loving look and noticed that Ed's leaves were all in a twist.

Ed, What Happened? Why Are Your Leaves In A Twist?

Ed unable to make eye contact could only droop and moan.

Ed, Please. Look At Me. Give Me Your True Feelings.

Ed sniffed, and wailed. It's Just. I Am Sick Of Being Stuck Here, Earl. Why Am I Always Stuck Here?

Earl paused before answering. Because, Ed, That's The Way You're Made.

But I Don't Want To Be Made Like This. I Want To Go With You!

Ed, You Can't Go With Me. You Have to Stay in the Ground.

But It's Not Fair! You Leave Whenever You Want and I Have to Stay Here And Feel Bad!

But I Thought— Earl retreated, hurt. Ed, Where Is This Coming From?

Ed's face was pained and contorted. I Just, I Hate That I'm Stuck Here While You Do Whatever You Want. Why Do I Have To Be The Orchid All The Time?

Earl knowing the answer brightened. You're Not The Orchid, Ed. There's No Orchid Here. There Are No Longer Binary Machines. Earl nuzzled Ed's center with her head and paused, thinking. The Problem, Ed, Is That We Have No Models. Insect-Flower Monogamy Is In The Minority, And Grossly Misunderstood By The General Public. How Can We Know How To Act?

I Don't Know, Earl. It Sure Is Hard Sometimes To Know How To Act. I Feel Like I'm Just Being Myself But Then Sometimes I'm Some Exaggerated And Flowerier Version of Myself Because I Think That's What You Want. But Do I Want To Be That? I Don't Know. Ed started crying.

Oh, Ed, You Think Too Hard. Earl softened her voice. Just Be You And I'll Be Me And We Won't Worry About Who We Want To Be Or Should Be. There Is No 'Should' Here. Only Us. No Object No Subject Just Us. Each Of Us Becoming The Other But Also Remaining Ourselves. Earl&Ed. She paused. But If It Makes You Feel Better, I'll Promise Not To Go On A Fly Unless You Agree To It. How Is That, Ed? How Does That Sound to You?

Ed breathed a perfumed sigh of relief and perked his petals up prettily. That Sounds Okay, I Guess. I Guess That Sounds Okay.

Earl bzzzed and bzzzed, and the two were one again.

*

The couple was again on solid ground. Ed felt more in control than ever, a new and good feeling for him, and Earl felt happy that Ed was happy.

Until Earl asked to go on a fly, and Ed said no.

Earl You Can't Leave, said Ed, wrapping Earl up in his leaves.

Please Don't Try To Control Me, Ed. I Need To Go On A Fly.

You Said You Wouldn't Unless I Agreed, said Ed. Earl You Hafta Stay.

I'm Not Leaving You, Ed. I'm Leaving To Stretch My Wings.

No, Ed pouted.

Ed, It's My Nature! We're Different! Put Yourself In My Wings. I Can't Take You Anywhere. How Do You Think That Makes Me Feel?

That's Not Fair, Earl. You Have Advantages That I Don't Have!

Exactly! And You Resent Them When You Should Be Admiring Them.

Ed scoffed. You Don't Admire My Advantages!

You Don't Have Any Advantages! Earl bzzzed furiously, battering Ed's leaves with her wings. She stopped, took a breath. I Think We Need a Break from Each Other. You're Too Dependent. She wiggled out of Ed's grip and flexed her wings. I'm Leaving, Ed.

Earl, No! You Can't! Ed clutched at Earl's wings desperately.

I Can, Ed, and I Have To. You Can't Go Anywhere and I Can and I'm Going To. Goodbye.

And Earl went for a fly and didn't come back, not for a long time.

Earl You Can't Leave, said Ed, wrapping Earl up in his leaves.

*

Ed not knowing what to do grew lonely. There was no way he could know where Earl had gone, or how long it would be before she returned, or if she would even return at all. He communicated with vibrations in the air directed at his neighboring plants in an effort to find out if Earl had been around. Having been shunned for choosing monogamy, he could gather no useful information.

Serves You Right, communicated Melpomene the distant azalea, For Screwing Up the Reproductive Food Chain. Wasphole.

Ed grew lonelier and lonelier and lonelier.

Earl How Could You Do This To Me. Earl I Wish I Would Die.

These were the thoughts running through Ed's head always and forever during this time.

*

Meanwhile Earl was on a fly, a very very long fly that allowed her to do some long and hard and needed thinking. She knew that things had gone sour but she also knew that nuptials could go sour and then turn ripe again. But sometimes nuptials went sour and stayed sour and never could turn back to ripe.

If Only We Could Be Ripe Again. But How Can We Know How To Do That? I Don't Know.

These were the thoughts running through Earl's head always and forever during this time.

*

The problem was that Ed was now long past due for pollination. Other insects stopped by hoping to join with him, but Ed unable to stomach the thought of another insect in his labellum closed himself off altogether from sex. Anyx the Butterfly would check in on him from time to time and inform him of any Earl sightings. Such sightings were infrequent and speculative at best.

Ed continued to miss Earl deeply and hard. But Ed was becoming sick of missing Earl, and so Ed decided to do something about it.

What might happen, Ed thought, if he stopped waiting around for Earl who might never return, and did something just for himself?

And so Ed decided to self-pollinate. His own babies would come from himself and he wouldn't need Earl ever again because he would have his own babies around him, his own babies keeping him company in the long cold nights. Anyx would make sure Ed's seeds stayed close and didn't get carried away by the wind, and Ed would have a family and become happy again.

*

Time passed, and passed.

Until one day while Ed was bending down lovingly to observe his children's growth, he heard a buzzing familiar and close.

Ed! Ed! I Have Returned, My Love, To Find You So Pretty!

Ed being astonished and thrilled that Earl had returned but also angry and hurt that she had left, did not know quite what to do.

The anger and hurt won over. Earl Fuck You. I Have My Own Family Now Who Stays With Me And Never Leaves.

Earl gasped. Only then did she notice all the slender new infant orchids peeking up from around Ed lovingly.

But Ed Ed I Love You! I Needed to Think And I Thought! I Want To Be Together! I Want To Start Over, Get Back To How Things Were!

It's Not That Easy Earl. It's Never That Easy And It Won't Be That Easy For Us. Ed swerved his body around with finality, refusing to meet Earl's gaze.

Earl went sadly away. She returned daily to try and try again and again. She made friends with Ed's babies, playing games by dipping and diving in circles around them until they were twisted together and shrieking with delight, with Ed looking on in amusement.

And Earl would say as she had been saying every day since her return, I'm Sorry Ed. Please Can You Forgive Me?

Finally Ed Junior and Isabelle and Yahweh and Iffie who were old enough now to understand the situation nudged and nudged at Ed, yipping and yipping until finally he could only laugh and spread his leaves wide for Earl to embrace them.

And so they were Earl&Ed again, and happy.

*

Slowly or quickly things became strained. Earl loathed parenthood, all these new threats to Earl&Ed. Worse, Ed could not seem to stop jabbing at her as punishment for her long leaving. Over and over Earl rolled around the question of how she could fix the situation.

Ed Let's Exchange Symbols of Love, Earl said one evening as the children were dozing off. Ed Will You Commit To Me For Life?

Ed's petals perked up. Then wilted. He knew what Earl was up to. He sighed. We Can't Use Symbols As A

Band-Aid Earl. They Won't Heal Our Wounds. They'll Only Hide Them. Besides—

Ed was interrupted by Iffie, who screeched, Yahweh Pinched My Buds! Instantly Ed turned from Earl and bent down to take care of his offspring.

Earl's wings slumped. Watching Ed scold his children with devotion, Earl at last understood. Ed didn't love her; Ed just wanted to never be left. Earl had been wasting all this time for nothing, nothing. Now all she wanted was an escape and to be alone. Earl launched forward, desperate to go for a fly.

Ed popped back up, indignant. Earl You Get Your Wings Back Here! You Can't Leave Unless I Tell You You Can!

Earl was sick of this argument as she had never been sick of it before. Earl had wings and could fly, and all Ed wanted was to clip them. So she left.

Ed watched sadly, saying nothing, as Earl's body faded into a dot and then disappeared entirely. He had no idea

Had Ed ever truly loved her?

where she went or when she would come back, or if she would ever come back at all. Maybe they had never really loved one another, he thought, if things could end this way.

Ed moved on with his life and reached a certain level of contentment by opening himself up to a number of trusted insects. But Earl lurked in his memory, his actions, in the way he formed his sentences, and when the weather was beginning to turn Ed felt the shadow of Earl's impending death intruding upon his happiness. Ed could not ever shake Earl off.

Nor could Earl shake the Ed out of her. She heard his voice in her head, and began taking on his characteristics: the way he shivered in the wind, the way he stuck out two petals when he talked. Had Ed ever truly loved her? Or had he only wanted company and affection? Though she wished to, Earl could not get over the demise of their relationship. In a faraway oak tree during the first frost she ended up freezing to death.

THE GIRL WITH THE EXPECTORATING ORIFICES

1.

Once I was seeing this girl I knew. One night she came on really strong, was the reason I started seeing her. I had received a text that said "help. Eiunk." I had called the next cab.

It was 2 or 3 a.m. in a late night goth club. I'd arrived to find her lurching out of the bathroom, having just vomited in the toilet. The vomiting was from mixing whiskey and absinthe, she explained. Too much whiskey, she reasoned.

Watery snot ran down her lip. She snuffled it back up and into her nostrils, where it rested for a breath, then went running down again, as she told me she was Very Attracted to me, with a wobbly smile. I offered her a Kleenex. She shook her head, hugged me hard. My t-shirt absorbed the snot.

The night we first attempted sex she had diarrhea several times before taking off her clothes. Nervous anticipation, she explained, only slightly mortified. She wanted it to go well. Soon she started crying, out of pain from her ravaged asshole. The snot came down again. Laughing overhard at her lunacy, she pissed on herself, then, during our fucking, which I commenced in an effort to distract her, ejaculated all over the bed.

She was so embarrassed by all of the liquids her body was expectorating, she started crying again, then laughing, and the cycle began anew.

It was like this for two months.

Twice during that time, she menstruated.

Artaud's screaming body is the original body without organs, screaming with suffering and the desire to end its suffering, though suffering is necessary for its survival.

The weeping body is similar, but not the same.

The weeping body is not important. What we have here is an expectorating body. This girl had orifices that expectorated at will.

Was the girl a trap? Would I fatally drown in her fluids? Is there a drowning that is not fatal? Why did she expectorate whenever I was around?

If I had answers, I would not be telling this story like a story, like this. Instead I'd develop a thesis.

Thesis: There is always a girl with expectorating orifices.

Though I liked her violently, was fully and wholly in love, I didn't know what to do with her, or with her body.

Though I also like violence, it was not a part of our relationship. She needed to be safe. She never felt safe alone, or in the streets which she said wanted to fuck her. I don't know how she lived her life from day to day when she was not with me. It's like that guy who had the enormous mutated colon, which contained thirty buckets of shit when he died, from a brain aneurysm. How did he live? But he did.

The girl I was violently in love with erupted all day, every day, and yet was highly functioning. She left home twice a day. She was on a tightly controlled schedule.

As much as I loved the girl and appreciated her extreme difference from others in the world, which made it seem like we were unique and beautiful soldiers whose passion for one another was more intense and worthwhile than any other passion in the history of the world or universe, I felt constantly guilty around her, as though the waves of fluid that erupted from her, that suffered her body, were my fault. Maybe they were.

The expectorating girl tried once to enter into violence with me. She told me she hadn't been straightforward, that she had had a boyfriend all this time, then wrapped my fists in duct tape and told me to punch her in the face.

Role reversal. I erupted in tears.

I was to leave for Germany in a few days. We decided to break it off.

2.

Deutschland. The trip marred before it began. I stewed with heartbreak and self-loathing, both states exacerbated by a festering wound under my nose, caused by the girl with expectorating orifices, who had chewed on my lips after vomiting, leaving a small cut filled with oral excrement, which had led to a mossy infection.

I was always absorbing her. She had told me her favorite novel was *Written on the Body*, which I absorbed on the train from Hamburg to Berlin. I decided she was giving instruction. We were participants in a sweeping and impassioned love affair. She was playing the role of Louise, the beloved, stuck in a dead relationship. I, the unnamed narrator-lover, was tasked with convincing her to leave. I would play the role I was given.

In Berlin, I met up with my first love, a filmmaker who was putting on an art show there. He was there with his boyfriend, who immediately started an argument with him about me. The boyfriend and I had arrived to the show at the same time, and the filmmaker had hugged me first.

It was Pride weekend in Berlin. We went to a club in the Kreuzberg district, where I ran into a dyke I knew from Chicago. She was a friend of a friend; we had sat next to each other during a movie some months ago. For weeks after, another friend and I had gone on about how interesting and attractive she was, and where could we find her again. And here she was, in Berlin, at the same night club, at the same time. She even remembered my name.

I would have gone home with the dyke I knew from Chicago, but for the expectorator being on my mind, and her mark on my upper lip, which hurt in addition to looking bad. Instead, I persuaded my first love, the filmmaker, to share his innermost thoughts. We were outside the club now, 4 or 5 a.m., leaning against the back of a doner kebab cart as the sun peeked into the sky. I told him about the expectorator, that I didn't know what was real and what was not; he took me by the shoulders and said, Make It Real.

His boyfriend, drunk, staggered out to swing a loose punch at my face. I dodged.

3.

I returned on the Fourth of July, the scab under my nose sloughed off to reveal delicate infant-pink skin. I sent the expectorator a swollen-hearted crossword puzzle explaining in cryptic fashion that I was still in love with her, what would we do? She responded with a poem. "Will not box," it started, and ended with an image of a volcano.

I knew what the poem meant, and didn't know what the poem meant, equally and at the same time.

When next we met, she gave me a firecracker.

Now I have placed a firecracker in the story, and know I must do something with it later, like next page, or the page after that. Perhaps I shall keep my readers guessing. Perhaps the firecracker will not go off.

In response, I wrote her a swollen-hearted cryptogram and left it outside her apartment in the pages of a book I had borrowed from her and read on various trains in various German cities. "[Name withheld] = W O U N D" was the key to the cryptogram. She herself was an open wound, I thought, not realizing this equation would wound her.

She wheatpasted a drawing of bandaged wrists to a stop sign in an alley. It is still there. Someone has since scrawled "Asshole" across it.

The asshole is another open wound.

Several days later, we met up one last time, declared our still engorged and festering feelings for one another on the couch of a club called Berlin. She started leaking again. Then she said goodbye, she was tired. I went home with someone else.

4.

The next week, I got a shield tattooed on my arm and entered into a relationship with the woman with whom I'd gone home. She was a bike messenger. She had a body like a citadel and a port-wine stain that crept up her arm and around her back. I wanted to fetishize her birthmark but didn't know how without making it seem like I only wanted her for her birthmark, which wasn't true. So I never said anything about her birthmark, though I ogled it often.

One night the woman whose body was a citadel did not text me back. Then the woman whose body was a citadel texted me back. I write this to make it happen. She has not texted me back but I want her to. To make the story real.

And it worked. She has texted me back and I have texted her back and so on. We have met up and met up and met up. We have watched television and had sex, shy and respectful sex with no firecrackers involved. She has given me a butane lighter, with which I can more easily light cigarettes in the wind tunnels on campus, and she has cooked for me multiple times, good, hearty, alien food.

I am passing as well-adjusted. Trying and failing, anyway. The woman who is a citadel has no patience for other people's pathologies. She is dismissive of mental illness, unsympathetic towards maladjustment of any kind. For me, this is new and refreshing. Past romantic exchanges have involved the glamorization of all parties' neuroses, which disallowed any falling away or healing.

All of this makes the citadel loom large and impenetrable. I lean in to kiss her as if she were my height, am surprised that her body is smaller. I open my mouth to speak, and a higher-pitched voice comes out.

Naturally I have stopped writing, although I am supposed to trade my novel with my writer friend in Philadelphia next week.

It has turned out that the woman whose body is a citadel also has a girl with expectorating orifices in her recent sexual and romantic past, a girl she'd had an affair with while seeing someone else. We've run into her at a club; I understand the citadel's attraction. I do not know what to make of this. By now I am Over the girl with expectorating orifices, though she is still Special in my mind.

I'm lying. I would almost certainly be with her again if given the opportunity. I imagine the woman whose body is a citadel feels the same about her own expectorating girl, and so I wonder what we are doing with each other at all.

5.

Now it is over. The woman whose body is a citadel has been emotionally cheating on me with her agoraphobic friend, and dropped me in order to deal with the impossibility of her love for this person.

This came from left field. I am stunned. Never had I realized the depth of the citadel's emotions. She had always seemed like stone to me, unyielding and vacant of pain.

Her agoraphobic friend suffers panic attacks, wheezings, inability to breathe in the outside world.

I also suffer panic attacks. All the time, in her bed, while the citadel was preoccupied with the agoraphobic's texts, I coughed and wheezed, my lungs in full stop. Was I allergic to her dog? So I said. But these were panic attacks. They set in two months into our involvement and didn't stop until we were done.

Certainly, my panic attacks are not as interesting as the agoraphobic's panic attacks. Here, the agoraphobic wins.

Prior to the coughing, I experienced persistent and explosive bouts of diarrhea for more than a week. This occurred immediately after realizing I genuinely liked and cared for the woman whose body is a citadel, but that she almost certainly thought I was Weird.

6.

My writer friend in Philadelphia kept her part of the deal. Here is a segment of her novel, about a girl named Jane and her failed relationships, which means it's about my writer friend and her failed relationships, and so about narrativity and performance:

> That night I got home early and I listened to the messages on the house phone and there was one from Lee. (Oh, hi, it's me. Sorry to call again. I can't reach you on your cell. I just thought I'd call because...I'm feeling...I'm...I'm kind of depressed, and I just thought maybe you could talk to me for a minute.) So the problem with this is not that Ben has a friend named Lee who still calls months

and months and months and months and months after they've broken up, nor is the problem that this is a girl whose naked picture remains locked in a secret box, nor is the problem all of the other problematic things that are obvious enough to forsake mentioning. The problem is that I know when he gets the message he is going to go running to her, and if I (his girlfriend) left that message he would say, everyone's depressed, Jane.

Jane, the narrator, is compelled by her boyfriend's ex-girlfriend's message to bludgeon the secret box open and set fire to the naked photos of Lee with rum and matches. The blaze gets out of hand. The fire department is called; there is a scene.

Ben comes home to this chaos, learns what has happened. Ben tells Jane she is crazy. Ben leaves Jane.

7.

I set fire to nothing. There are no photographs of the agoraphobic friend that the citadel has ever mentioned to me, which doesn't mean they don't exist. Still, I had every intention of lashing out. I planned to fuck the citadel's bike, take pictures and send them to her via cell phone, to slash her tires and so on. But I would give her one last chance first, to apologize for the way she had treated me, during the end of things. And she did. She apologized. Now I can't hate her. I can't fuck her bike. This, for me, is sad.

And so it has gone the other way. The desire that the citadel has developed for her agoraphobic friend makes me want her, miss her, more. All this time of not talking openly, she had been experiencing real and valuable emotions that I was not privy to.

The vice versa is also true. I am a wealth of real and valuable emotions. I wonder, if the citadel had known this about me, had known all of the things that make me interesting that I do not, did not tell her, would she have dropped me so soon?

Why is the agoraphobic so interesting? Why? Why? Why?

My friends tell me I should try things again with the expectorator. They've seen us together, they say, they've seen how we work.

But they don't understand. Now I'm the expectorator. I am crying and wheezing and shitting and puking and there is no one around to absorb it.

8.

Tonight I attended a lecture given by a professor who has written a book called *Obsession*. From his book:

> I am sure as I write these words that countless people all over the country are...engaged in obsessive-compulsive activities like cleaning and checking, fighting off intrusive thoughts, addictively thinking about sex, food, alcohol, drugs as well as acting on these addictions. ...Many folks are addicted to their nightly television shows, to collecting things, or to obsessing about that someone who is unattainable or lost forever.

Why is the citadel so interesting? Why? Why? Why?

In Latin *obsessio* and *possessio* were two aspects of besieging a city....If you've obsessed a city, you've surrounded it, but the citadel remains intact; while if you possess the city, the walls have been breached and you've conquered the citadel and its citizens.

I could not conquer the citadel. I could not breach her walls.

But. Once. There was a night I almost did. I stayed inside her apartment when she went out to walk her dog. Intending to wait in her bed, I entered her room and found a journal spread on her pillow, its pages erupting in poetry: lines detailing calloused fingers, a woman's back. Coming upon this gave me a jolt. This person who can hang a joke on anything was writing poetry in earnest? I did not recognize her at all.

Oh. Yes. There was another time, earlier, worth mentioning. This was a week after she'd been in a terrible bike accident, only a few weeks after we'd met. It was early still, barely nine p.m., and she was so drunk I had to pick her up in a cab. Once at her apartment, we ordered pizza; she ripped off my clothes. In bed, after sex, I asked her about the accident again, expecting the usual Yeah, Glad I Was Wearing My Helmet. But this time she started crying, sobbing, expectorating. She sat up and hugged herself. She wailed: It Hurts. It Hurts.

I embraced her; I did my best. I wanted so much to shield her, then, to be the repository for her vulnerabilities. But she was already shielded, and who am I to protect someone? Anyway, that was the end of that. In the morning, she was embarrassed, and claimed to remember little. I kept these things to myself.

9.

She broke up with me in a text message. She had moved on; I was not worth a conversation. When finally I persuaded her to speak with me, to explain to me what had happened, she told me about the agoraphobic friend, and I told her about my plans to fuck her bike if she had bailed on our post-relationship chitchat. She laughed nervously, said I was crazy, and okay, she was glad she had shown.

Was I crazy? Don't we all do stupid things, just for the thrill of doing them? Don't we all play our parts as they unfold? Was the citadel so immune?

In my end-of-relationship conversation with N, my last cis male partner, the one who was passing as feminist, the one who chased me for a year before I agreed to be dragged into his open relationship, he called me "empirical," "childish." He already had a ragingly feminist girlfriend, he explained, so when I refused to let him burn me with cigarettes, I had lost my purpose in his life. He'd found another lover, I learned later, who would allow him to burn her with cigarettes.

Prior to breaking up with me, N had written a story in which I recognized him in the protagonist and myself in a secondary character. In the story, the protagonist is an alien who "jumps" bodies by having intercourse with them and then turning them (mostly women) inside out. My character, who was described with my features and mannerisms, my habit of rolling my eyes whenever he attempted to dominate me, was one of the ones turned inside out, her entrails and innards grotesquely exploding all over the place. Her death was the bloodiest and most violent of them all.

After N explained our new friends-only status to me in condescending detail, I excused myself to use his bathroom. There, I stole his Zoloft.

At a bar a few days later, N called his new lover a bitch, burned her wrist with his cigarette, and punched her in the face full on.

10.

The night I blew off sending a draft of my novel to my writer friend in Philadelphia, my novel, cut up and tacked to a bulletin board, fell off the wall. This happened while I was in bed with the woman whose body is a citadel.

The night I failed at working things out with the citadel, the butane lighter she had given me fizzled weakly to its death.

I have since thrown away the butane lighter, and returned to my novel. It is no longer falling off the wall.

That is a lie, above. I have not returned to my novel. Instead I have been writing this, and that, and some other things.

I have never set off the firecracker that was given to me by the girl with expectorating orifices. Perhaps the firecracker, muffled and contained in my bag all these months, has lost its potential to explode.

Fuck the firecracker. Notice all the carefully placed fists flying. It is as though the punch the expectorator invited, but did not receive, has traveled through this story to land on N's new lover's face. This punch is what glues things together.

Ha.

The truth is I didn't try relationships until I was twenty-six and this story is a record of my adolescence.

Also it's been a way of making myself feel interesting after having been dumped for really the first time.

TRAUMARAMA

A Collaboration

This piece appropriates the form of *Seventeen Magazine*'s "Traumarama" section. Some of these narratives are based on or were influenced by my conversations with others about their experiences; some have been written by those who experienced them; some are found; many are fictionalized; all have been anonymized and edited.

Best section by far. Melissa would bring the new issue [of *Seventeen*] to the bus stop every month, and we'd go straight to the Traumaramas. The boys made fun of us but you know they loved it too. One time Eddie pulled me aside to ask what a wet fart was like it was some secret girl thing, and I had to make something up because I didn't actually know! I guess the word 'shart' had yet to emerge in the popular lexicon. Anyway there was one [a wet fart] in each issue, usually ruining someone's lavender prom dress. And there was an early period, and someone tripping and spilling soda all down their shirt so their bra was visible, and someone's dad walking in on them shaving their crotch. The same ones every month, a humiliation machine. We loved being unimpressed too. Like oh, you walked into the volleyball net...and a *boy* saw it! Come on. We wanted the most humiliating things imaginable to happen to other girls. —S.J., 28

I think they really equalized us. I mean, I felt so awkward and gross all the time, a pimply blobfish floating the halls. The Traumaramas were a relief. I wasn't the only one who'd made eye contact with a cute boy and promptly fallen down the stairs. I wasn't the only one who'd imagined Chad's note for Stacey could actually be for me. All of the Staceys had done these things too. —M.T., 31

Of course they were all made up—by the staff writers if not the girls themselves. During sleepovers, we would stay up concocting the worst Traumaramas that could ever happen. It's funny, we totally knew the formula—some sort of bodily exposure or malfunction, a cute boy or "major hottie" to witness it, a humorous quip at the end—but we were so naïve and, well, uninventive that the best we could come up with was an orthodontics mishap that's probably physically impossible during a sexual encounter that's also pretty unlikely. It went something like: "I was with my husband in our hotel room on our wedding night. I was soooo nervous giving him a blowjob for the first time...and then his condom got stuck in my braces! Now every time I give my new husband a blowjob I'm" —wait for it—"braced for disaster." —C.M., 28

This is an excellent distraction for a rainy Sunday! I've been pondering your e-mail in the back of my mind for the past few days, and really haven't been able to come up with anything show-stoppingly/jaw-droppingly/gleefully good. But here's something, for what it's worth: When I was in grammar school, I was speaking with a classmate by the sinks in the bathroom, and was so engrossed in the conversation that I mindlessly attempted to follow her into a bathroom stall, upon which time I was called a lesbian. So for the longest time I thought being a lesbian meant a) not being cognizant of the natural end of a conversation or b) someone who liked watching people urinate. —A.D., 25

It was 1997. The first Lilith Fair. I was wandering the grounds and reveling in the queer camaraderie when I spotted the woman of my horny teenage dreams. She sat sobbing by herself on the edge of a fountain in the cobbled square where vendors were selling hemp yoni necklaces. She couldn't have been more than 22, but I gotta say, it took some brass ovaries for a 16-year-old to do what I did next. I sat down next to her and asked what was wrong. I nodded, oozing concern, at the same time stroking her hand and shooting her bedroom eyes. Little did I know, I was also oozing something else. When it became clear the woman wasn't the Sapphic sister I'd hoped, I gave her a lame little platonic hug and retreated back to our spot on the lawn. As I knelt down to sit, I caught a glimpse of my crotch. It was my "Moon Time." The Goddess had summoned forth my womanly essence all over the back of my khakis. The stain was shaped roughly like Africa. Not exactly the smooth loverboy look I was going for! —G.S., 29

I was speeding on my way home because I was about to have diarrhea so bad, I mean really bad, any second, and of course I get pulled over. I stop and I yell at the cop, "I know I'm speeding, I gotta go shit! Follow me to my house!" So he does, and he parks in the driveway with the lights going and gets the paperwork started while I race inside. I take my shit and I come out, and he's like "Hey... did you go to Gretchum High?" It was Rob, that guy from Spanish. —K.S., 33

So I come home from my first semester in college and I learn that my mom has found my private journal and read it, and she's corralled the entire family into confronting me about my unholy perversity. My family is a family of God, and I had been journaling extensively about my repeated attempts at autofellatio. Awkward!...I confessed to substance abuse. Not only did this divert their attention away from my exciting masturbation life, it also provided my mother with something more palatable to moan about with her church friends. —C.A., 27

I went to Miami my first spring break in college. One night we were at a bar and I was chatting with a guy who bought me a drink. So I drank it. I started feeling woozy, so I excused myself to go to the bathroom. I was able to get my pants down and sit on the toilet but then I lost my ability to move. Something was seriously wrong. I couldn't even move to get up off the toilet. After a while my friends found me and helped me up and sort of dragged me back to our hotel. I know, my bad for drinking a drink I didn't buy myself. I'm just thankful I was smart enough to recognize something was wrong and get myself out of the situation before—you know, I don't even want to think about it anymore. I wish I had a story about tampons or something. —L.F., 32

When I was 22 I was seeing this girl and every time we fucked she had a tampon in, which I felt was not right, but because I hadn't had a lot of sex and she had, and because she was incommunicative and kind of scary, I decided to make sense of it in the way that we all make sense of things that don't make sense, through rationalizing. Maybe she likes the feeling of getting fucked with a tampon in, maybe it extends the feel of the fingers, maybe she is an ejaculator and the tampon absorbs the mess. Then one night I encountered a tampon in her vagina and it was slimy and gross and I knew with horror that it must be always the same tampon. I stopped and asked her about it but she kept dismissing me, saying I was only feeling

the powerful muscles of her cervix, so I shut up and kept fucking her. This happened the next night too. (She was really scary, you don't understand.) Finally I couldn't take it anymore, I was having nightmares about TSS, it had to stop. So the next time we were fucking I didn't ask, just coaxed out the tampon as gently as I could. It came out soaked and shrunken and stinking of stale band-aids. We both stared at it, silent, until in one motion she jerked out of bed, scooped the lump from my hand, and ran shrieking into the bathroom to dispose of it. Of course she'd had no idea it was there, and who knows how long it had been there, and meanwhile I'd known about it for two weeks and hadn't pressed the issue because I assumed I didn't know anything. We were equally mortified, I think.
—L.O., 26

Last summer I went to a queer dance party with my girlfriend, who can get a little insecure when we go out, because I'm very social and outgoing, and she's reserved and prone to jealousy. It's an ongoing problem that we're both aware of. Anyway, we were all having a good time I thought. I was dancing with my friend Dara and just having fun and my girlfriend comes over drunk. She grabs my waist and slurs all this crazy shit about how I'm flirting with Dara and making a laughingstock out of her [my girlfriend] in front of everyone. I laughed because it was so ridiculous. Well, that just made her angrier and she hit me in the face. Obviously this does not fly in any space, but in a queer space, it's particularly bad, because there has to be all this processing afterwards. The organizers made her leave and told me she wouldn't be welcome there ever again and that they would make sure I felt safe there, which was cool of them. But then the next day they send out a message to the *entire Facebook group* of like 800 people, attempting to process the violence and to reaffirm their safe-space policy. So now everyone—and these are people I *know*—thinks I'm some battered woman who's staying with a shithead who beats her up, which is not true, this was the first time anything like this had ever happened. And you know what, I love this person and she's absolutely mortified by this moment, this one stupid mistake, and she's apologized repeatedly and she's agreed to go to couples counseling and take an anger management class and curb her drinking, all this stuff. But my friends are all *judging* me like I'm some passive victim who's too weak and codependent to get out of my abusive relationship. It's just like, aaaahhhhh! —J.B., 29

I had a bunch of friends over one night and my roommate was the only hetero in a group of lesbian- and queer-identified women and to her this meant she needed to adamantly assert her love of cock, mainly to be controversial. She just would not shut up about cocks— "real cocks, not the plastic kind." It was getting annoying and finally she was just being outright insulting to us, saying crap like "you don't know cock until you've tried it, ladies, really you don't know what you're missing," as if none of us had ever fucked a cis dude before, and it was so dumb and I shouldn't have taken the bait but finally I just told her to shut the fuck up, and she told me to shut the fuck up, and this went back and forth for a while, our voices rising and her getting aggressively in my face and then something went off in my brain and I hit her. I smacked her in the head in front of everyone and then I ran into the house embarrassed. —N.R., 27

Hey friend! I am excited about this project and looking forward to reading what you come up with, but not feeling up to excavating old humiliations right now. I know you and others find sharing cathartic and necessary, but I don't deal with things similarly. —A.G., 38

There are two genres of embarrassing slash humiliating stories I could tell you—one that is kind of funny and does not reflect badly on me in any way—and the other that is actually embarrassing and lessens my social capital. So the ones I'll tell you, you probably won't find interesting enough to use. I don't think I've experienced anything that I would call truly traumatic. —A.W., 30

Honestly, I have so many I don't know where to start. Okay. So I had this boyfriend who said the weirdest things. Once after I got on all fours on his bed and he stood behind me and fucked me with his fingers, and after I'd come, and he'd come, and I'd come again, this time begging for more fingers, he smiled and said pleasantly, "Mildly kinky, eh?" Another time, and I don't remember if it was before or after that, I had read about talking dirty in a book my friend gave me, so I was talking dirty to him while I rode him, and I was doing this baby voice, and flipping my hair around, and I thought I was definitely his fantasy right then, especially when I said, "I love it when you make me c-c-come," and he (again) smiled and said pleasantly, "Everyone enjoys sex." So I shut up and just kept bouncing. I think it was a different time, but same position, I was approaching my theatrical climax—which was good but not that good, but I wanted to be his fantasy—so I was trying to sound like a little girl but also knowing and experienced and in charge of my own sexuality but also all gaspy and awed and surprised, when I of course farted, this quacky little duck-call fart, and his eyes got all big. He didn't have any grins or choice remarks about that one and it's the kind of thing we should have laughed about, and normally I love to laugh about farts, but that time I was grateful he pretended it didn't happen. —J.H., 28

Oh, wait. There's more. The boyfriend before that was finger-fucking me once, and he suddenly stops, and I look up, and there's this look on his face of absolute horror, like he's just reached into the Cracker Jack box and gotten a fistful of vomit. "What?" I ask him, and I'm kind of terrified, because what could make him look like that, there must be something pretty wrong, do I have herpes? and he doesn't say anything, but he shows me his fingers, which have some brownish goop on them. I figure I must be spotting—it's at the very very end of my period—and he doesn't know what that is, so I have to explain THAT to him as well, and he basically doesn't accept it. This should not be happening, he says. Then he says, "Can't you just squat down and shake it out?" I really can't get him to see that it doesn't work like that, and he goes to wash his hand, with soap and great personal offense. Months later he says to me, "Remember the time there was all that old brown blood trapped in your vagina?" This same boyfriend, I got pregnant with him, and he was pro-life (or whatever it's fucking called) so he wouldn't come with me to the clinic or take me to the hospital when I had a bad reaction to the anti-nausea drug they gave me but he definitely did not want me to have the baby, but sometimes he would poke my belly and say, "Baby in there." I know it sounds like I'm trashing him, but the real joke is on me, because I was dumb enough to get pregnant a second time with this guy, deny it, wait for him to figure it out and dump me, have the abortion (uh-gain) by myself, make chitchat with the abortion doctor while she vacuumed out my insides, chitchat about a creepy professor of mine she knew from the gym, someone she considered a close personal friend, someone who whipped his shirt off in front of boys he liked during office hours and propositioned the head of the department, made chitchat with the doctor while staring at a goddamn inspirational poster with a picture of a hot air balloon on it and some bullshit about "There are no mistakes," made chitchat until it really began to feel like I was being raped by this thing vacuuming me out because I felt it displacing my organs and pummeling my belly sick the way it happened when I had actually been raped, on a weird pseudo-date, the year before, and that's the point when I stopped making chitchat and yelled at her to stop it right now, just stop it please, and she said OK, and she did stop. This same ex-boyfriend said he was against lesbianism because his sister had OCD and mentioning lesbians or things lesbian-ish triggered her. And I told this guy I loved him, a bunch of times. —J.H., 28

There's not one event. It's this shapeless ghost that travels with me, and it takes forms in all kinds of ways and when I least expect it. There are triggers, yeah, but sometimes I can't predict them. And often I have to do the work of reassuring whoever I'm with that it wasn't them, it was just this thing that happens sometimes. It's this whole cycle. Like, I could contribute to your piece but I probably couldn't read it without going down multiple bad head trips. —S.M., 27

I was on the train going home, sitting and minding my own business listening to my iPod and looking out the window considering whether to make quinoa salad or a veggie burger for dinner and suddenly this dude's hand's between my legs. I was too shocked to move or say anything and I just sat there for a long while, not breathing, not protesting, not stopping it in any way, not looking at him, not looking at his hand, in total denial that this was happening, instead fixating on the familiar whine of Taylor Swift. The person in front of me had long dark hair that was draped over the back of the seat with one strand hanging loose from the rest. I wanted to reach out and pull that strand, it was all I could focus on. Then the bell for the doors rang and snapped me out of it and I got up and pushed past him to get off the train. When I told my friends later they made a big thing out of it and I shrugged it off, no big deal. But it was. —B.Y., 26

I think that having it fictionalized or not quite right is almost more hurtful than sharing it with people. And it's also almost more hurtful if were anonymous and not attributed to me. Because I own it. You know? And that's the hardest thing. I own it and it took a long time to own it, to acknowledge it. Even just acknowledging that these things happened to me, that took years. And it's not just me who was affected. Getting a reputation in high school, that's not just me who had to deal with it, I have a younger brother and sister who had to live with that too. I guess I've always thought that I would do something good with it. Like work at Planned Parenthood and tell girls who want to have an abortion it is okay. Tell girls who have been raped that they are somebody. They will become themselves. I know you're an artist and you can do whatever you want but I don't know. This is mine. —J.D., 32

A former partner of mine had a really brutal experience as a kid that she wouldn't tell me about. I mean she would occasionally refer to it to explain certain reactions to things but she wouldn't tell me exactly what happened. Even though I knew it was a bad experience that she didn't want to relive, I was a little loopy one night, maybe a little drunk, and I made it into a silly game, like I was trying to get her to share some juicy but benign secret, like who's-your-crush, tell-me-tell-me. What-was-it-what-happened-can-I-guess-if-I-guess-right-will-you-tell-me, I went in a singsong voice, like it was fun. I'm so ashamed. She tolerated me for a few minutes with what I realize now was an embarrassed smile, embarrassed for me, I mean, and then she looked me straight in the face and said, firmly, No. —H.P., 28

SWAMP CYCLE

KILL MARGUERITE

I am in the swamp which is dark and murky. Another character is with me in the swamp and a stink of infection breathes thick around us. The stink is repeating more broadly the stink of the pussing wound on my toe, which came from stumbling around in the swamp. There was a rough thing in the swamp last night; now, a pussing wound on my toe. This wound would be classified an abrasion. We have been moving along on the solider peat to keep my toe from ingesting the swamp which is a breeding ground for all kinds of things.

Another character is with me in the swamp and I have to take a shit. Before I can take a shit I'll have to admit needing to take one to the other character. This breeds anxiety but I can do it because I have to.

The other character is my father. I broach the subject, cheeks aflame. My father transmits disapproval with a hateful sneer. He says we must get out of the swamp; this is our first priority.

But I have to go to the bathroom, Dad. I have to take a shit.

The shit can wait, he declares.

But I would be more comfortable, I protest.

Can the shit wait? he asks in a rhetorical question, shutting down any response but he's right. I have already slowed us down with the abrasion.

I am defeated. We walk on.

The air is growing cold. The pus on my toe is hardening. The swamp floor is cold, and damp, and sludgy. Soon it will be too cold to want to take a shit. The cold air will make my skin tremble and my asshole shit-shy. Is the asshole a mouth or a gate to another world? A question neither rhetorical nor answerable.

The shit will be enormous, I think to myself. It is knocking on my gate and wants to get out. It is taking up space in my body that might go to something else, like positive energy. I need it to be outside of me. If only my father agreed with my needs.

With moist and urgent gurgles, my bowels clamor for their contents' release. I need my father to be my friend.

My father is now my friend. I tell her I must do it, take the shit, now. My friend nods and smiles appeasingly, but looks ahead with clenched jaw. My friend is grossed out and also wants to get the fuck out of the swamp, because of a few motivations, but she is kind of a pushover and will do what I say.

There is no path off of which to move, so I squat down straight in the swamp. My friend moves away to allow me privacy, and also to move away.

When I take the shit that I need to take, the shit is black and heavy and curved; and ridged, the shape of its bowels.

Waste moves inside me. Organs move inside me. After the shit, a membrane. My bowels are creeping out. I need my friend to be my father, because I have something to prove.

My friend is now my father. He fixes his face away. I want to gloat since I knew I needed to take a shit, and now there is proof I was right. But my father refuses to witness the shitting: my triumph is stuck in the air.

My father's propriety stinks. While he stalks about ignoring me, I watch my bowels ooze out, inside out, curving forward so that I see the results of my actions.

At the end of my protruding bowel tube, which seems odd because bowels do not really end but connect to the stomach; but this bowel tube has an end. It ends in a nipple.

I lean over, grab my protruding bowel tube, and raise it to blow on the nipple.

This means sex.

I need my father to be my lover. My father is now my lover. My lover comes over and crouches before me, dropping trou and spreading ass cheeks in front of where I am squatting and staring at my excrement. My third nipple guides my excreted bowel tube into my lover's asshole, whipping through his intestines instinctively. My protruding guts rub on the skin of my lover's guts. My bowels slide in and out. In and out. Stay.

My guts are swelling to fill my lover's guts, and the intensity is too much to bear. I need to detach. My third nipple clamps down on the end of my lover's bowel tube with its teeth. Then it swiftly retracts. In so doing, it rips my lover's bowel tube from his body. He shrieks and falls to the swamp floor, our intestines drooping between us.

I no longer need my lover. The swamp sucks him down. He's gone.

My intestines retreat partially inside me, leaving the nipple extended, still gripping my lover's guts in its mouth.

The swamp burps.

We walk on.

I am in the swamp which is dark and murky. A stink of infection breathes thick around me. The stink is repeating more broadly the stink of the pussing wound on my toe, which came from stumbling around in the swamp. I have been moving along on the solider peat to keep my toe from ingesting the swamp which is a breeding ground for all kinds of things.

My toe aches deep. I imagine the parasites and bacteria that have wormed their way into it. My toe throbs anew at this thought.

I need to stop and tend to my toe.

My third nipple lets go of my dead lover's bowels, which drop between my legs to the swamp floor. I pick them up and wrap them around my toe. I tie them in a bow. My toe is soothed. The bubbling stops.

I wish the other character were here to witness this transformation, as the wound was a sore spot between us. But the other character is gone.

I miss them. I want an other character.

I hear a moist and urgent gurgle, and experience a momentous shift in my gut. An enormous weight ejects itself, pummeling through a dilated and yielding esophagus. I vomit up this weight, and look what I have vomited.

It is an other character.

We have made life.

My third nipple again comes alive. I need the other character to be the baby. The other character is the baby. The baby shrieks. I hold its mouth to my third nipple. It latches on. I lift the baby with the nipple in its mouth and hold the baby in my arms. This is the first I have seen the baby in perspective. The baby is normal looking, I guess.

The baby sucks my bowels.

We walk on.

Around us the swamp lurches, heaving with the stink of shit and rusty afterbirth. After a stretch of sucking, the baby begins to howl. The baby howls and howls. I suspect she may be constipated.

You seem uncomfortable, I observe. Do you need to take a shit? I position the baby on the peat. Sure enough she begins to shit, though not without great difficulty.

The baby's face is red and blotchy from being born and is becoming redder and blotchier from the difficult shitting. Her shit is like a balloon that squeaks from her anus in an excruciating sound. She looks at me panicked. I, too, am alarmed. The shit is too large for her asshole. Her asshole needs to be my father's asshole.

The baby is now my father. My father is taking a shit and not looking at me. Though I know he is my father, I will treat him like the baby because that's what he needs.

Good work, I say to my father, who is no longer crying or panicked but comfortable in his skin. You feel better now. Later he will be embarrassed.

My father is now the baby. I make funny faces and she squirms on the swamp floor giggling. I pick up the baby and settle her on my hip. This swamp may never end. We walk on.

ACKNOWLEDGMENTS

My grateful acknowledgments are extended to the editors of the following journals and anthologies in which portions of this manuscript have, in various forms, appeared:

"Circe," in *Pocket Myths: The Odyssey*.

"Slug," in *Fist of the Spider Woman: Tales of Fear and Queer Desire*, Arsenal Pulp Press; and in *The &NOW Awards: The Best Innovative Writing*, Lake Forest College Press.

"Kill Marguerite" (chapbook), Another New Calligraphy Press.

"Tomato Heart," *The Wild* Vol. 1.

"The Girl with the Expectorating Orifices," *Everyday Genius*; and *Lit Magazine*.

"My Father and I Were Bent Groundward," in *Thirty Under Thirty: An Anthology of Innovative Fiction by Younger Writers*, Starcherone Press.

"Dionysus," *PANK: The Queer Issue*.

"Earl and Ed," *Monsters & Dust*.

"Twins" (chapbook), Birds of Lace Press.

"Swamp Cycle," *Artifice Magazine*.

"Floaters," *Red Lightbulbs*.

"Traumarama," *Projecttile*.

Thanks also to Cathy Nicoli, who interpreted and performed "Tomato Heart" as a movement piece at Amherst College in 2007; to Jessica Grosman, who performed "Slug" on Montreal's CKUT's Audio Smut show in 2009; to my editor, Bryan Tomasovich, who shrewdly and enthusiastically helped shape this book, and all at Emergency Press who have supported the project; to my family, who must not be confused with the characters in this book; and to Leeyanne Moore, Christopher Grimes, Lidia Yuknavitch, Kate Zambreno, Judith Gardiner, Gene Wildman, Lennard Davis, Samuel R. Delany, Sandra Newman, Joan Mellen, Andrea Lawlor, Abbi Dion, Lily Hoang, Davis Schneiderman, Alexandra Chasin, Amber Dawn, Johannes Göransson, Cynthia Barounis, Gabe Sopocy, James Share, Rachel Bockheim, Jenn Hawe, Libby Hearne, August Evans, and Anne Derrig for their contributions, feedback, and support.

Emergency Press thanks Frank Tomasovich
and Jill and Ernest Loesser
for their generous support.

Recent Books from Emergency Press

Road Film, by Ernest Loesser

There, by Heather Rounds

Gnarly Wounds, by Jayson Iwen

First Aide Medicine, by Nicholaus Patnaude

Farmer's Almanac, by Chris Fink

Stupid Children, by Lenore Zion

This Is What We Do, by Tom Hansen

Devangelical, by Erika Rae

Gentry, by Scott Zieher

Green Girl, by Kate Zambreno

Drive Me Out of My Mind, by Chad Faries

Strata, by Ewa Chrusciel

Super, by Aaron Dietz

Slut Lullabies, by Gina Frangello

American Junkie, by Tom Hansen

EMERGENCY PRESS

emergencypress.org
info@emergencypress.org

Megan Milks lives in Chicago. Her work has been included in *30 Under 30: An Anthology of Innovative Fiction by Younger Writers; Wreckage of Reason;* and *Fist of the Spider Woman: Tales of Fear and Queer Desire*, as well as many journals. She is the editor of the anthology *The &NOW Awards 3: The Best Innovative Writing*, and co-editor of the volume *Asexualities: Feminist and Queer Perspectives.*